Ballard Branch

# HER ADULT LIFE

NO LONGER PROPERTY OF
SEATTLE PUBLIC LIBRARY

# *stories* HER ADULT LIFE

## JENN SCOTT

ACRE

CINCINNATI 2017

Acre Books is made possible by the support of the Robert and Adele Schiff Foundation.

Copyright © 2017 by Jenn Scott
All rights reserved
Printed in the United States of America

Designed by Barbara Neely Bourgoyne

Library of Congress Cataloging-in-Publication Data are available at the Library of Congress.
ISBN-10 (pbk) 1-946724-02-5 | ISBN-13 (pbk) 978-1-946724-02-1
ISBN-10 (ebook) 1-946724-05-X | ISBN-13 (ebook) 978-1-946724-05-2

No part of this work may be reproduced or transmitted in any form or by any means, electronic or mechanical, including photocopying and recording, or by any information storage or retrieval system, without express written permission, except in the case of brief quotations embodied in critical articles and reviews.

The press is based at the University of Cincinnati, Department of English and Comparative Literature, McMicken Hall, Room 248, PO Box 210069, Cincinnati, OH, 45221–0069.
www.acre-books.com

Acre Books books may be purchased at a discount for educational use. For information please email business@acre-books.com.

# CONTENTS

# HER ADULT LIFE

# NARRATIVE TIME

A day passed, and another day.[1]

1. Morning coffee. The girl with the green scarf wrapped too tightly around her head drinks her coffee black. She wears the green scarf because she wakes each morning looking superficially like Einstein: electric hair, shock of white skin, dilated pupils. She wakes looking like a replica of herself in a grainy black-and-white photograph with sharp distinctions of shade; like a cardboard cutout in a store window, hovering against a pane of glass while children knock their fists against her two-dimensional knees.

In the cafe, she drinks her coffee black. She reads, glancing up between sentences, breaks of words, letters. She wonders why it's necessary, these breaks, such space. It is too easy to escape into the emptiness between things. She imagines herself crouched in the fat hollow of an *O*; imagines her back pressed against the rounded stomach of a *D* as if it is the glistening hood of a car, her pale chest beckoning the sun. She stares at Murray Avenue in the bright morning light, toward the dark interior of the as-yet-unopened liquor store. She stares at the crazy woman, ostrich neck straining, letting the dog out of the illegally parked car while its owner leans into the cafe's granite counter, purchases a pound of whole bean Sumatra. Beside him, Stripper Lawyer with his chest like Ken's holds the tiny handle of an espresso cup before bending over the girl with the green scarf's notes. He exclaims over her penmanship: "Such tiny, beautiful writing! Look at the way you fit two written lines inside each printed line. You should get that analyzed. Then again, maybe you shouldn't!" He laughs with closed lips, tilts his head back to suggest something uproariously funny.

I

"I'll refrain," the girl with the green scarf says.

"Back when I was in law school, stripping to pay my way through, I would have killed for writing like that!"

Behind Stripper Lawyer, the woman from the real estate office is interrupting, nudging the shoulder of Stripper Lawyer, who has abandoned his espresso cup to tug at his slick ponytail. As if in response, the woman from the real estate office smooths her own hair, so forcibly blonde the girl in the green scarf waits for it to scatter like a dandelion, abandon her scalp in a single gentle explosion. Brother Floyd, the crazed black man with his red bow tie and too-small suit, yells to the barista above the whir of foam materializing. "I need money for deodorant! For the smell, Danielle, for the smell!"

The woman who wears the winter coat in summer heat sits in the girl with the green scarf's favorite seat (third seat from the door, closest to the counter and its pitchers of free tap water with swollen floating lemons). The woman who wears the winter coat in summer heat circles her hands around the warm comfort of a coffee cup, stares for hours at nothing in particular. Her winter coat resembles the flotation device found beneath the seat of a plane. She alternates her palms between the comfort of her coffee cup and the squatness of her purse. Occasionally, lifting her hands from the sweaty brown leather, she glances at the girl with the green scarf triumphantly, and this glance says plainly: *I am sitting in your seat.*

In the morning, coffee. The girl with the green scarf reads sentences twice, three times over. She flips to see how many pages are left in the chapter (thirteen), listens politely as people stop to speak to her. They bend over her table, her book, her coffee growing ever cooler. On the sound system, the *Braveheart* soundtrack begins anew.

Stripper Lawyer smooths the slickness of his ponytail, tells the girl with the green scarf about his experience with a psychic last week. "She said I had a thirteen-year-old son! I thought she was crazy, until I remembered the woman from college who told me she'd had an abortion."

"Whoa," the girl with the green scarf forces herself to say.

"I'm serious," Stripper Lawyer says.

"Me, too," the girl with the green scarf says. "Whoa."

"We should go out sometime, maybe get some sushi."

"We should, except I'm really busy lately."

Stripper Lawyer swipes a renegade hair. "Aren't you unemployed?"

The woman who wears the turban slides closer in the seat beside the girl with the green scarf. Her breath smells intensely of garlic. "Please, come over tonight! I make a lovely dish with fava beans!"

The girl with the green scarf says, "It's fall. Fava beans have been out of season for months now."

The woman who wears the turban says, "I'm very handy with beets. Also, with potatoes. I make a very delicious apple-and-barley salad."

"I have a hard time digesting grain."

"I've seen you," the woman who wears the turban says. "You eat far too much sugar. You have a pallor, like you're not getting enough B12."

The Philosophy PhD candidate with the yellow teeth says, "I'll mark these seventy papers today if it kills me. It will probably kill me. I stand a better chance against polio. Not sure what you people in the English department are doing over there. These students can't construct sentences to save their lives. What have you been teaching them, besides nothing?"

"I am no longer actually, specifically, part of the English department. Your insults no longer apply to me."

"And anyway, why are you reading that book? His ideas are vague, useless." The Philosophy PhD candidate's arms flutter up and away in a demonstration of uselessness.

The woman from Library Science drinks her third mocha. Her hair explodes like a nuclear burst above her head. She says, "I can't fight a two-front war. I can't fight a war at home and a war at work. I can't have a husband like that and a boss like this." She clacks a spoon inside her glass before standing to emphasize her point. "Do you understand?" she asks the girl with the green scarf, pounding the table to emphasize her words. "I can't have a husband like that and a boss like this!"

The insane mumbling man at the table beside them, drawing maps across an endless supply of napkins, stops drawing midline to say, "Woman! Stop complaining and get your body out of my face!"

Coffee. Cream and then sugar, raw, poured any way but carefully from the dispenser. The girl with the green scarf needs comfort, cream's fat rounding coffee's sharpness to curves. She has found solace in the most unlikely allies: Leeza and the never-ending investigation into murder and rape. Montel and his obsession with paternity testing. ("This is ninety-nine percent accurate and admissible in a court of law.") The news. ("Traffic and weather together.") Sports with the sportscaster her gay friend had sex with.

"Terrible, absolutely terrible in bed!" her friend said. "Beer cans scattered everywhere, and the entire house smelled like piss!"

The girl with the green scarf believes the sportscaster squints his left eye at her. He knows that she knows that he's poor in bed, drinks too much alcohol. He knows that she knows the length of his afternoons, all that exhausted endlessness. She knows that he has sat across from a lover, wanting only to touch a strand of his hair, an earlobe. He has thought, mistakenly, that an earlobe could be enough. His lover has said to him, "You're too fragile," and the sportscaster slept with him anyway, knowing the comfort of this single night was something he might draw out like taffy. She considers telling his face projected in the television screen, his neck gawking, the pimple on his chin, his tie slightly askew: nights like that are akin to glass, too delicate and easy to break, moments containing nothing but the clarity of themselves.

The woman who wears the turban drinks tea and says, "Personally, I think it's easier to abstain from sex. Think of the trauma the vagina undergoes every time!"

The girl with the green scarf says, "No, please, I'd rather not."

Stripper Lawyer drinks espresso, stands laughing with the woman from the real estate office. His laugh is too loud, the laugh of a crow. This morning, his ponytail is drawn back so tightly it gives his face the impression of a facelift.

"He has a line for everyone," the woman who wears the turban says, with a nod toward Stripper Lawyer. "He had a line for me, if you can believe it."

"He constantly wants to have sex," the woman from Library Science says.

"Your boss?" the girl with the green scarf asks.

"No," the woman from Library Science says. "My husband."

At home, the girl with the green scarf watches the newscaster bumble the Steelers' coverage. She suspects that he, too, eats peanut butter out of the jar for dinner because this is all he can muster. He, too, calls his mother, who tells him, "I tell you all the time not to call during *Dallas*. I can't talk during *Dallas*."

"*Dallas* ended years ago. It was a dream."

"I'm watching it now. Only one season was a dream. The rest was real. So don't call me."

The girl with the green scarf suspects the sportscaster's mother has heard him crying over the phone and asked, "And what is it you expect me to do?"

Morning coffee. The girl with the green scarf counts six pages until the end of the novel. She imagines what happens in the white spaces, those decided narrative pauses. She imagines the protagonist bored. She imagines her watching too much television, eating too many doughnuts without brushing her teeth afterward. Running the vacuum, taking baths with salts, visualizing success. The girl with the green scarf understands no one cares what happens to the protagonist in the white spaces. She understands that she is jealous of her, trapped inside her narrative with its convenient elision of time, its smoothing over of days and weeks and months to the decisive moment, the place where the action unfolds.

"Lucky bitch!" the girl with the green scarf says to no one in particular, perhaps to the woman from Library Science, perhaps to Brother Floyd, perhaps to the woman who wears the turban, whose turban she helps fold on the cafe's frozen patio with the tables and chairs piled high for winter. They fold the turban corner to corner, corner to corner, until it is a square the woman who wears the turban can shove inside her bag. The girl with the green scarf is not sure why they have folded the turban; the woman who wears the turban's shaved head stares up at her, demanding to be covered. There is snow.

The woman who wears the turban says, "Please don't say the word *bitch*. No woman deserves to be called a bitch."

Or maybe the girl with the green scarf says these words to Stripper Lawyer, standing beside her in a new suit with a dizzying array of pinstripes, a newspaper tucked into his armpit: *Lucky bitch!*

"Did you strip for that suit?" she asks, trying to make a joke. "Or litigate for it?"

"You used to be so attractive, even with the scarf. Now what? Too many books?"

The girl with the green scarf tries to discern: he is making a joke, he is not making a joke. Stripper lawyer steps closer, touches a finger to the dark crescents beneath her eyes that have come to resemble craters on a distant moon: first one, and then the other. She does not have the energy to tell him no, don't do that.

"Oh," she says, and it occurs to her to wonder: how long ago was it that she might have said something different? How long ago was it when she might have chiseled out the sharpness of a response, hurled it at him like a discus?

Standing above the table third from the door, closest to the counter, Stripper Lawyer touches her lips. He smooths their roughness with fingers that smell curiously of sardines, and she believes, in this strange, looming moment, that he will kiss her. She lifts her chin toward him. Behind them, the *Braveheart* soundtrack crashes out a crescendo. She imagines Stripper Lawyer pressing her against his ironed slacks and suit jacket and kissing her, right inside the café like a scene from some golden Hollywood movie. Some terrible and distant part of herself wills this. Some small and quivering part of her thinks, *please.*

"Hmm," he says, turning from her before choosing instead espresso, the steady and dependable print of this morning's paper.

# HER ADULT LIFE

Kate is telling Michael the story of the knife.

This is the knife, she reminds him, they bought together at the kitchen store on Forbes Avenue, back before Kate began cutting her fingers on the cruel edges of manila folders for a living and long before Michael got so sardonic. That was a time in their lives when they were young enough, naïve enough, to believe that thinly-stemmed martini glasses and hundred-dollar fondue sets would give their lives a feeling of feigned grandiosity. They were both drunk on this particular occasion, having just sucked down several gin and tonics apiece at The Squirrel Cage, despite the fact that it was scarcely midafternoon. Kate had grabbed a stockpot for support inside the store's compacted aisles while Michael grabbed her sweaty waist, steadied her, saying, "Whoa, there, whoa," as if mistaking her for a piece of prized livestock.

"Right," Michael says. "The knife." He sits on her battered couch, coddling his beer and plucking lint from in between his toes. Smelling of hops and nicotine, he brushes her bare legs with his flannelled chest as he leans over the coffee table for a cigarette, and Kate considers whether this brushing is accidental or decidedly logistical, something covert and in need of dissection. She hopes to discover, in reminding him of this story, that his voice carries the pink tinge, the translucent swell, of nostalgia, but his words are instead succinct, not quivering, unemotional. He has the stony jaw, the hardened aloofness, of someone used to listening to the ill-formed ideas of college students.

Kate spent nearly two hundred dollars on this knife primarily because she was drunk and in possession of her very first credit card, but also because her sister, in the thick midst of a life crisis and recently graduated from the culinary institute, had said forget knife sets, specifically those advertised on QVC in the early morning viewing hours. A real knife, she said, speaking in her professional voice with its forced dramatic pauses, was a chef's knife, preferably German and with a stylish insignia. What Kate chose that day in the store was a cleaver, Japanese and made of pounded steel so light it could have been Excalibur. She'd handed her credit card to the store clerk, whose voice had the pitched lilt of encouragement, while Michael's face hung above the cash register like a persistent satellite. His arm had found its way once more to her waist, and they had taken the cleaver into their possession, silently suspecting, she was sure, in the rosy, rash way of youth, that long term, *in the end,* they would be together.

James, upon seeing this cleaver lying in its box on the kitchen counter, shrouded in tissue, had asked simply, "What the fuck?" Kate was with James then, as she had been since the dawn of time, since *before* the dawn of time, but Kate guessed one day she and Michael would love one another. She guessed they would chop things and have intellectual conversations over foie gras and paté, neither of which—Kate now acknowledges—needs to be chopped. Back then, Michael had loved her with the intimidating, unrelenting passion of youth. He'd appreciated her inconsistencies and flaws, her mood swings and chiseled angst. Around her, he tended to be hotheaded and furious. He drank black coffee and smoked cigarettes. He ate ramen and left the window shades down and wrote poems involving various combinations of these things.

With this knife, she says, for the first time in her adult life—her kitchen life, she might call it, her domestic life—Kate chopped her way through squash, through carrots and eggplant, with the same ease with which she had previously decided to butter toast, yet again, for dinner. The knife she'd had previous to the cleaver had been her mother's, discarded after Kate's sister had professed shock over the astonishing dullness of the blade. *The real cuts occur with the dull knives,* Kate's sister had told their mother—this as Kate's sister had been reduced to breaking parsley with her fingers when it should have been finely chopped, and the statement had seemed to Kate a profound bit of metaphor, ominous and upending. Kate had been then twenty, a junior in college. She had just moved into her first apartment and her brand of cooking did not necessitate knives but rather countless varieties of frozen ingredients that seemed to have taken a vow, cross their hearts, never to go bad. Kate opened the cans and plastic bags these things came inside; she reheated them. Occasionally, if she remembered, she stirred them with a sense of satisfaction and afterward licked the spoon, causing her sister, if she happened to be around, to lecture about bacteria and proper kitchen hygiene.

"Pre-cleaver," Kate tells Michael, "I spent twenty minutes once, slicing potato."

"Your point?" Michael asks.

The story of the knife unfolded yesterday, moving day. James stood before her, tanned and smiling in the June sun, pleased to have interlaced the arms of chairs and legs of tables for maximum spatial capacity, thereby managing room for her papers, the black halogen floor lamp that everyone in America seemed to own, the standing mixer that had recently caused a great deal of tension between them. Who, after all, got the stand mixer? Kate called heads, and she, in this instance, got the stand mixer.

"I am a true technician," James said. "A Jesus, the Messiah of moving."

"That doesn't even makes sense," Kate said. "That reference is faulty."

In the afternoon light, it looked as if he had not washed his hair for some time, and Kate pointed out that this, perhaps, was his single similarity with Jesus. Unfortunately, *this* Messiah forgot to lock the back doors of the moving van. At the intersection of Forbes and Murray, a cacophony of horns surrounded them when they pulled up to the white line.

9

"Do they mean us?" Kate asked.

"They do not," James said, "mean *us*."

They had meant them. When James pulled the van to the side of the road to lock the doors, Kate mourned the loss of her answering machine, a box of cheap wineglasses, several undergraduate English papers, and a pink ceramic teapot she'd made junior year of high school, the single thing she'd made in crafts class that hadn't exploded in the kiln. She'd had the initial inclination to hold this teapot protectively in her lap as if it were a kitten, but James had lodged it beneath her orange lampshade slowly losing its shape beneath the crush of objects and said, "It's a *teapot*." Kate did not like the implied meaning—the derogatory stress, she would have called it—on these three words. "It's under control," he had said, and she wanted to circle back to this point—the point of his absolute control—when she discovered she no longer possessed either a pink teapot or an orange lampshade.

"He's disappointing like a Messiah," Michael says now. He has switched over to jug wine, which he is drinking from a coffee mug. He exhales a puckered mouth of smoke.

Kate knows that James is not a Messiah of anything, despite whatever passionate claims he might make. Certainly, he is not the Messiah of moving objects of any sort. He once loaded a bookcase into her car in such a way that the awkward pressure of one corner against the windshield caused dozens of hairline cracks to shoot across the glass as they drove down the highway. "That's beautiful," he said, having stopped the car to examine the situation. "Look at that." This occurred not long after he'd taken her car to have a flat tire repaired but returned with a smashed passenger door from the accident he'd had while running a yellow light on the drive home. "The most important thing," he'd said, prefacing their walk to the car. "The thing you really need to remember is that you no longer have a flat tire and that no one is dead."

Michael says, "You never ask the person who's asked you to move out to move you."

"I know that," Kate says. "I do."

"You clearly don't. What, did you think that under the stress of moving, he might rediscover his love for you inside a box marked *kitchen?*"

"We ate dinner together," Kate says. "We actually ate dinner together."

After moving they had, in fact, decided to eat one last meal together, as if to prove they were adult enough to masticate and converse in one another's presence. They went to that place in the Strip, the Caribbean restaurant with its conch fritters and fried plantains, the faux thatched roof covering the dining room. There, they had the same incompetent waiter as always, with his terrible shirt replete with faded images of palm trees and lounge chairs, the occasional piece of lone tropical fruit: lone banana, lone papaya, lone mango. There was little conversation between them save the exclamations James gave to the spotted silverware, the small chip at the base of the stemware, the unidentifiable fleck in the curry aioli accompanying the yucca fries. What Kate supposed was meant to be Jamaican music splintered from the speakers above them like something dropped repeatedly on a hard surface. The waiter stared dismally into the dining room from his waiter's station as if trying to remember something. When Kate's fish arrived overcooked, James shook his head at her when she asked to have it redone.

"You're crazy if you expect me to eat overdone tuna! But okay, fine, whatever!"

"Ah," he said, sucking the last of his drink. "Tuna martyrdom." Sitting across the table from her, he looked wan, sallow, pushing around the paella on his plate as if it carried the weight of a severe snowfall. Even his hair seemed to have lost its verve, its erect enthusiasm for life.

"How are you?" she asked, abandoning the issue of the fish. She was momentarily regretful that she was not the sort of person who hoped the best for him, that she was not the sort to think, well, as long as he was happy.

"Wonderful," he said.

Kate searched this answer thoroughly, checking it twice, three times, for irony. Finding none, she discarded it quickly.

"How's Mary?" she asked and regretted she was not the sort of person who actually cared how Mary was; she did not actually hope the best for Mary.

"Mary," James said, "is very good."

"I'm so glad!"

The pivotal moment came, Kate says, when he eschewed dessert. He refused to order it despite the fact that this was what they always did: he ordered dessert, and she ate it. It seemed to her a cruel psychological blow, that he would not order dessert as a sympathetic last gesture toward their relationship.

"You could have ordered it," Michael says.

"That isn't the point!"

"You're old enough to order dessert if you want it."

"You can't even be depended on," Kate had found herself saying when the Hawaiian-shirt-clad waiter left the check, "for something as inconsequential as bread pudding."

"The key words," James said, "the words you should really pay attention to are *inconsequential* and *bread pudding.*"

"Is bread pudding too parochial for Mary?" Kate asked. "Mary prefers things like brûlée and sabayon?"

"Christ," James said.

"What, Mary prefers the organic qualities of a galette? A pie is too rigid for our girl Mary?"

"I've been thinking," James said.

"What's that?" Her voice had a decided drunken edge to it. It was something she might cut her thumb on. She felt guttural and German, too broad in the shoulders.

"That everything I've ever felt about love until this point, this moment right now, has been superficial."

"Are you forgetting?" Kate asked. "Those eight years spent with me?" She remembered meeting him, in blinking sunlight, the very day she'd arrived at college. He'd worn a Volvo mechanic's shirt with a name patch on it that read *Bud* and smiled condescendingly at her when she'd admitted liking a certain hardcore Hare Krishna band.

"Actually, I have those in mind," James said.

"He actually said that," Kate says now, pouring herself a mug of jug wine.

"I can't imagine why," Michael says.

"Who did I buy a two-hundred-dollar knife for?" Kate asks. "Who did I cut all those potatoes for?" She imagines herself huddled over the snatch of counter inside her and James's claustrophobic first kitchen, industriously slicing potatoes with an undeterred, masculine aggression. She might have well been logging trees in the forest. She might have well been wearing orange, a color branding her for easy rescue.

"You eat potatoes," Michael says. "I've seen you."

They'd driven home sullenly. Or, Kate sat sullenly in the passenger seat, and James drove, occasionally lifting his hands from the steering wheel to improvise guitar solos to the especially bad songs on the radio, a habit Kate had always found annoying. When she finally lumbered out of the $19.99 moving van, she was crying. Kate was crying and simultaneously imagining the sad sight of herself crying. She was realizing slowly, like an accumulated drip, that this pathetic sight would be the last image James would have of her. She never made an attractive sight when she cried. She never looked dainty; she never inspired others' tenderness toward her. She always looked too red, too much like a puffer fish. People tended to look startled when they saw her crying, as if she'd just been punched in the face. Crying, she leaned over and slid the cleaver from the car dash into her purse, the delicate crocheted one James had given her several years before for no reason other than a simple kindness he clearly no longer possessed.

"Why," Michael interrupts, "was the knife on the dash?"

"I told you," Kate says.

"I would remember a knife on the dash. You said nothing about a knife on the dash. You said this was a story about the knife, and this is the first I'm hearing of it."

The knife was on the dash, Kate says, because James put it there, having deemed it improperly packed. Rushed, she'd slid a drawer full of kitchen things last minute inside a plastic bag, everything at once—measuring spoons, can opener, wine bottle stoppers, box of nails, cleaver. When James hoisted the bag inside the van, the cleaver poked out of the plastic and drew a fortuitous scratch across his arm. She could not have drawn a cleaner scratch across his arm if several strong men pinned him down while she tried scratching his arm with a cleaver. His blood appeared brighter and more ostentatious than she remembered it, like a piece of her grandmother's costume jewelry. Together, they located a towel, and James applied pressure, something he insisted on doing himself because he no longer trusted her interpretation of pressure. As a result of all this, he'd set the knife on the dash so that he might keep it in plain view for the duration of their time together. She'd forgotten about it until after dinner, when she noticed the knife resting on the dash, demonically reflecting the light from the streetlamps as they drove.

"You know that's a bad place for that," James had said as Kate, crying, slid the cleaver from the dash into her purse.

"I'm leaving," she said, "and you're thinking about a knife."

"I'm thinking about your extremities," he said, "and hoping you won't lose them."

Kate slammed the van door, then, and ran off. She wondered briefly in her flight if James would follow her, but she saw, turning to watch him from behind a hedge, that he drove away without so much as the single sidelong, wistful glance she'd hoped for. Kate watched the van take its first sharp left away from her. *This,* she tells Michael, is why she went to the wrong house: because it was dark out and because she was crying. She was immersed in the drama of her own crying, as though watching it on a grainy projection screen, and in this immersion—it felt cold, like an improperly drawn bath—she went to the wrong back porch. She didn't immediately realize this, though it occurred to her as she manhandled the key inside the lock that her porch furniture looked nice on this porch, dainty, until she remembered she didn't own porch furniture, least not of all this porch furniture: white wicker hugging sweetly floral cushions, like something borrowed from the Walton family. Also, she did not own hanging plants, despite her appreciation of their seeming tranquil domesticity. Her experience with wind chimes involved glancing at them in nature stores, just as she glanced at the walking sticks, fleetingly, wondering why she was inside a nature store in the first place. She'd never actually owned a wind chime, but here were several hanging listlessly from the eaves next to several hanging baskets.

"Why were you going through the back door, anyway?"

"The front key didn't work," Kate says. "The landlady was recopying it."

It had occurred to her with a quick flutter of embarrassment, like something caught beating its wings at the nape of her neck: she was on someone else's porch. This was someone else's back door. She was *trespassing*. She was a *trespasser*. She felt a clammy moment of panic, at first cool then hot, before she turned very quickly to leave and in this process knocked several ceramic plant containers off the porch railing and onto the cement driveway below. They shattered with brilliant clarity as Kate, desperate to escape, started down the porch steps and, in her haste, missed several on her flight to the driveway. She fell palms first onto the concrete below, hitting it less dramatically than the ceramic pots, but still with a sudden loud *thwack* that jarred her entire body. She lay there for what seemed a long time. She pressed her cheek against the concrete and felt momentarily frightened, incriminated in something terrible. The moon, when she finally cricked her head in its direction, looked misshapen and too bright.

She picked herself up and ran.

"Did you find the right house this time?" Michael asks.

"Haha," Kate says, and it is a dry laugh that sounds like coughing.

When she got home and fumbled through her purse in search of some small comfort, a chocolate or a mint, it struck her: the knife was gone. It occurred to her with a sick feeling that the knife was at her neighbors', most likely on their porch. She considered simply leaving it there; walking away, forgetting the entire situation. She didn't necessarily need a knife. But she'd paid over two hundred dollars for it, and this knife was a symbol of her adulthood, her newfound independent domesticity. Without this knife in her possession, she might doom herself to failure and disappointment, a lackluster destiny. Also, she could not help envisioning her neighbors' startling discovery of the cleaver the next morning, perhaps lying at the threshold of their back door, sharp and ominous in the daylight despite the fact that she'd never bothered sharpening it with the steel gadgetry the store clerk had convinced her to buy. She had to go back for it.

"*She had to go back,*" Michael says, sounding like a movie voice-over.

It was very dark when she made the trek across the brief stretch of stubby lawn. Unfortunately, the neighbors did not have motion lights. They did not have lights at all. She tripped her way along the periphery of their house and up the porch stairs, where she immediately dropped on all fours like someone in an evacuation exercise, sliding her hands around the slats and grooves, sweeping her fingers here and there, carefully, so as to avoid getting splinters. Then the porch light snapped on, and Kate found herself flooded in light. She blinked and made herself smaller, but noticed immediately: her neighbor stood in the open threshold, watching her. The neighbor was wearing only his underwear, briefs that looked unnaturally white in the darkness. He adjusted a golf club unconfidently in his right hand and faltered forward.

This all happened, Kate tells Michael, very quickly. As soon as she registered what was happening, before she could stop herself, she was standing up and running down the steps, over the concrete, through the stubby grass to her house. Her neighbor's voice punctured the air behind her, gained momentum. "Hey, hey. *Hey!*"

She did not stop until she made it safely to her house, the right house, where she locked the door behind her and slid over the chain. She saw her hands were covered in residual dry blood from scraping them against the concrete. Examining herself in the bathroom mirror, she saw that she must have at some point touched her face: her cheeks had several dried red smears, like war paint.

"You're not laughing." Kate acknowledges Michael, staring at her too seriously over the cigarette he's just lit. Catching her eye, he turns his attention instead to the swell and retreat of the embers as if they are something mesmerizing.

"It's not funny."

"It is, too."

"It's troubling."

"It is not," Kate says, "*troubling.*"

"You could have just talked to him. He's your neighbor. You could have been neighborly." Michael's voice has the sound she dreads: dreary and intellectual, as if scratching itself. His eyes have the same lazy, condescending, bored blink of cats' eyes.

"It's funny," Kate says. As if to emphasize this point, she touches Michael's knee. She squeezes it, ever so gently, and when she does this, his entire leg jerks forward, as if like a doctor Kate has just checked the responsiveness of his reflexes. She feels emboldened by this, the fact that she has touched his knee. Knees are delicate, wonderful things. They're smashed and ruined every day; they're fragile enough never to recover. She thinks that she will kiss him. *Knows* that she will kiss him. He has waited years, perhaps, for this moment. She notices, sitting so closely to him, that even his lips have the wistful scent of tobacco smoke she previously attributed to his flannel shirts and dirty jeans. And then, she is pressing her wet lips against his dry ones; is accidentally catching a front tooth on his bottom lip. It occurs to her that possibly she can be too forceful, but before she can rectify this situation, he has turned his head abruptly so that she receives a mouthful of his sandpapery jawline.

"Whoa," he says, swiping at his lips with the side of his hand. "Whoa, there."

"I thought," Kate begins.

"We're not kids," Michael says. "We're older, not as stupid. I'm not stupid."

"What does that mean?" Kate asks.

"You know," Michael says, evasively, and Kate has no idea. She wants to be young, younger. The beauty of being young was, in fact, the ability to project all that might happen. She recognizes, suddenly, how less grandiose the projection of her plans has become. It's like she was once standing looking an expanse of field, but now she's trapped in a hallway hung with too many pastel prints of landscapes that refuse to interest her. It's as if she's moved her entire life inside a dental office, minus the gas that sings a person to sleep while their cavities are filled, their roots fixed. She doesn't even have that happy, wonderful gas. She doesn't even have Michael, sitting uncomfortably beside her, still looking at his toes in an attempt to locate some pleasant distraction that might take them firmly away from this moment, here, happening between the two of them.

She does, however, have her knife. It's in her possession, tucked beneath a cereal box on top of the refrigerator for safekeeping. She doesn't tell Michael this. It strikes her that this would be what he was most interested in, this part of the story. He would be most interested in her need to omit such a thing. She knows what he would say, in between swift drags to his cigarette and in that voice that annoys her. *Omissions give meaning to what actually exists. Gaps create meaning.*

The truth is, just this morning, before she left for work, her neighbor—the neighbor—rang her bell. She opened the door, and there he stood, no longer wearing underwear but instead dressed and pressed for morning. She was, unfortunately, still wearing pajamas. She had not yet washed her face. She was terrifically not coiffed. At the sight of him she sucked her breath in deeply, incriminating herself, but before she could say a word, he was handing the cleaver to her swathed protectively in a dish towel, an ingenious idea, she realized, something that had never occurred to her when she was stuffing it inside a garbage bag.

"This belongs to you," he said, and Kate knew that she was supposed to say something. She was supposed to utter something reasonable or logical, but she could not bring herself to speak. She stood for a long time in silence, staring at her neighbor, who in return stared at her. Somewhere in the kitchen, the coffee maker exhaled steam. Kate shifted her weight to her opposite leg. Minutes passed. Or maybe they hadn't been minutes at all but terrible, elongated, and exposed seconds that seemed to her an eternity, an entire dismal lifetime. And then, when Kate still had not said anything, the neighbor pivoted, tracing his steps back down the walk and disappearing as if he'd never been there in the first place.

And really, now that she's thinking about it, Kate doesn't know if she's making it up—the particular odd quirk at the edge of the neighbor's lips, his smile hovering but never, in fact, materializing. She did not know what it meant that he would not just smile, but that he was caught in this state of not smiling, this state of lingering and watching. She'd thought possibly she heard the intricate rattle of his brain as it registered the subtle and surprising, the disappointing, pieces of her. These were the pieces she could not see; these were the pieces she could not speak. She faltered under his steady gaze, and in her nervous exposure, did not thank him for returning her knife. She did not thank him.

# LESSONS IN GEOGRAPHY

On the night of the Russian daughter's arrival, they had abandoned Marcus's car at the bottom of the street and crawled uphill on all fours to their apartment because they could not balance on the thin sheath of ice that was the road. They were improperly dressed, snow alighting on the bare crowns of their heads. Claire thought this was something they should laugh about: ha, ha, ha. She thought laughter might serve to warm them. It might tighten their stomach muscles and prove to them they were two people with senses of humor, how remarkable.

"Ha!" Claire laughed into the cold. "Ha, ha!"

"Right," Marcus said. "This is funny."

Marcus frequently poked fun at the literal quality of Claire's laugh. She laughed and it sounded, literally, like *hee, hee, hee* or *ha, ha, ha*. He knew the *hee, hee, hee* was the genuine version of her laugh, while the *ha, ha, ha* was its neurotic cousin. Marcus's own laugh was an open-mouthed laugh that probably looked inviting to things that did not often have access to mouths. He laughed and beat his hand against his knee as if he wanted to pound his poor, abject kneecap into submission. He had once been very generous with this laughter, as if he'd happened upon a large shipment of it and felt forced to endlessly dole it out; his was the black licorice of laughter. Crawling up the hill, however, Marcus did not laugh. He looked like a badly crafted figurine. On her own hands and knees, scraping her way slowly up their street, Claire felt ferocious and beautiful in the wind, untamed, like an animal listed on the verge of extinction, but Marcus ripped holes in the knees of his only adult-looking pants.

"The point is," Claire said when they were finally inside, shaking off the quick remnants of melting snow, "you should have more than one pair of actual pants."

"Whatever," Marcus said, sounding petulant, like someone had taken his lollipop from him. On the television, a news commentator spoke from inside her shapely wool turtleneck. *Please, avoid shoveling snow into the road! The snow trucks are doing the best they can.* A second commentator interjected, *Viewers! This is tonight's poll question. Call, please, with your opinion: does the city neglect the secondary streets?*

"I have my opinion," Marcus said, "about this city and its secondary streets."

Outside, Claire stood close as he shoveled snow from the walk purposefully into the road. His cheeks appeared bright red, ripe with something unidentifiable that she wanted to scrape off and examine inside a petri dish. He shook snow from the thick folds of his scarf, sipped the bourbon he'd carried outside in his coat pocket. He shoveled around her feet and asked with a thin tightening of his voice, "Do you *have* to watch?"

Claire was not actually watching Marcus. She was waiting for Joe and the arrival of the Russian daughter, though Claire would never admit this. Waiting for Joe. Joe lived across the street. He was her friend, and such people, Claire knew, were hard to come by. He visited her at work, and she gave him the overbaked and underbaked pieces of things, the sugar flowers that had lost their luscious bloom, the stale meringues that Claire liked to crush into powder beneath her slip-resistant heel. He brought gifts endearing in their simplicity: a plastic pastry blender from the dollar store, a ratty wooden spoon from the thrift store. They took drives together, ticking off the names of places they finally reached and saying, *We've been here now, here.* They drove toward the borders of neighboring states, and it shocked her to hear: Joe had never been to Ohio or West Virginia. He had never been to New Jersey. He'd left Pennsylvania twice in his lifetime, once to live in Texas with his first wife for the brief, harried two years of his marriage, and again to meet Elena in Moscow. Claire sometimes imagined him living in a beige tract home in Texas, standing in a yard whose grass had gone to seed, unaware that some twenty years later he would travel to Moscow to meet his second wife, Russian but a great deal softer than that first—kinder, gentler.

Marcus found Joe two-dimensional, like a Colorform, though he claimed not to be biased. He would say this about any man who thought a mail-order bride was a viable option and whose favorite possession was an oil painting of himself and his dog. Marcus could not help mentioning this painting with an italicized rhythm: "What kind of *man* hangs an *oil* painting of himself and his *dog* above a *mantel*?"

"Would you feel better, darling," Claire asked, "if it were acrylic?"

In this painting, both Joe and the dog had the drooping faces and chins of people who had recently inherited money and begun taking themselves too seriously. They appeared too erect and proper, too squared; it was uncomfortable to look at. Recently Joe had replaced this painting with several framed snapshots of Elena and Elena's daughter. This was what people did, Claire understood, when they declared themselves committed to one another. They rearranged and reorganized. They cleared out space. Joe was going to marry Elena; the necessary conditions had accumulated like drippings in a pan. Elena was taking English classes. She was learning to talk pleasantly about the weather, to describe objects in terms of their color and size. *The dog is big. The man is good. The painting is weird.* She took driving lessons every Saturday. She met with her Russian group to discuss the complications of American living. Claire suspected Elena cooked cabbage soup and borscht for dinner and that Joe ate these things with an unmistakable male fervor that said he'd made his commitment, he'd eat cabbage soup and borscht forever, for the rest of his life, so help him God.

"The Russian daughter arrives tonight," Claire reminded Marcus.

"Great," Marcus said. "Wonderful."

"Don't forget," Claire said. "Tomorrow night. The party."

"No, thank you."

"There will be lots of alcohol," Claire said. She added, "I've always appreciated your ability to assimilate under duress."

"Is that band playing? If I have to hear his cover band," Marcus said, "I'll die. He's a drummer, but he has no rhythm. It's like you waking up one morning and deciding to drum."

"It's like you," Claire said, "abandoning sarcasm altogether."

"That," Marcus said. He leaned heavily on his shovel. "Will never happen."

Claire never told Marcus: she kissed Joe. She kissed him a year ago, pre-Elena, during Joe's annual winter house party at which she'd felt uncomfortable and too young. The partygoers were mostly middle aged, lingering against walls with feigned nonchalance and fondling their beers with the kind of whimsy with which they'd like to be touched. She stood for a long time in a corner of the basement, drinking gin with wild desperation and thinking of Marcus, who liked to say in his way of crystallized condescension, "Gin is a summer drink." A man stared lecherously as she moved between mixers. Several middle-aged men plucked dishearteningly at guitars, whacked at a drum set.

"There's this woman here," Joe said, intercepting Claire on the basement staircase. His breath came at her, thick with alcohol. "My friend's wife. She just came from Thailand."

"You mean, a mail-order bride."

"She's his *wife*."

"Vaguely," Claire said. "Don't get any ideas."

"Claire," Joe said, leaning close to her. "You're so negative."

Claire thought this kiss was something she would soon forget. It reminded her of the heady newness of her first kiss, experienced in her parents' basement while the family photos stared at her, evaluated her technique. At the surface Joe's kiss had had a train-wreck quality to it, and beneath that, a tentative sweetness Claire realized was foreign to her. His hand rested just so on her left hip. He understood the concept of pressure; she hadn't known pressure had a concept. She thought pressure was just pressure.

Their single sexual encounter occurred on a Sunday afternoon, post a devastating Steelers' loss. It had become clear the quarterback couldn't throw from the pocket, scramble and improvise though he could. He was sacked. He threw interceptions. Someone, after the game, dumped a Coke over his head. An important linebacker strained a groin muscle. The post-game analysis had an angry tone, something like an insistent drumbeat, while Joe fumbled busily with Claire's shirt buttons. His lips grazed her chin. He kissed her, and she could not get Meatloaf out of her head. *Like a bat out of hell I'll be gone when the morning comes. When the night is over, like a bat out of hell, I'll be gone, gone, gone.* John the dog sighed uncomfortably beside the bed, gnawed heartily at his tail. Intimacy seemed then beautiful and strange. It involved pale skin and sweat and fear, bumbling insecurity, starts and pauses, apologetic monosyllables. The fact that they could share something like embarrassment seemed profound, meaningful indeed. The fact that she could survive embarrassment gave her hope that she could be a different woman than the woman she was: kinder, gentler, complacent and fat. That she was not necessarily a hard, angular person, someone to measure strictly with a ruler. Though she was this person in relation to Marcus, if surrounded by other people, she might, in fact, behave differently. As this other woman, she would wear sweatpants and forget to shave. She would love a man easily, in a not afflicted way. She would sing for no reason: in the shower or at work, as egg whites spun about in the mixer, slowly attaining their peaks.

In the aftermath of their sex, Joe appeared too erect and proper, thoughtful, as if working out the mathematical equation of his body related in time and space and distance to her own body. He never stopped making this calculation, a complicated word problem he wanted desperately to resolve but could not: he was forty-four years old, she was twenty-five, that left how many years between them? She'd met Marcus when she was eighteen. Now she was twenty-five. That meant they'd been together how long? She and Marcus were the same age. This left no necessary calculation to speak of, but seemed important to him nonetheless.

She did not tell Marcus any of this. Marcus was not a jealous person. He didn't get angry, though Claire would have preferred that he was the embarrassing reactionary type who punched walls and left scenes of destruction around him like villages he had pillaged and set fire to. She sometimes imagined him screaming at her in a crowded restaurant, smashing plates and demanding to be loved by her. In these dreams, his voice always sent a flurry of women following her to the bathroom. There, they dabbed tissues at her eyes, soothed the nape of her neck. *Ahh, dear,* these women always said, smelling like lilacs and powder. *Ahh, darling.* But this was not Marcus. This was not the person he was.

As for Elena, Claire had believed that she was not a person at all but simply a notion Joe was entertaining, the way he might consider learning to blow glass. He spread the catalogs across Claire's kitchen table, and Claire laughed: *ha, ha, ha.* She had read somewhere that laughing was good for the abdomen; hers was a beautiful abdomen, indeed. In these catalogs were skeletal, bikini-clad women who clutched kittens; or those who leaned against trees, hair askew, as though they'd conquered a fit of wind. Elena intimidated Claire because she appeared normal. Hers was a snapshot, a Polaroid, unassuming. She was appropriately sized: a person could hug her and feel satisfied, in the end, that he'd accomplished something. Her personal statement was perfunctory. Her soul was not an issue. She did not bead things, or crochet, or care for the sick or elderly. *I look for husband and home.* She had, Claire pointed out, a seventeen-year-old daughter. She did not speak English.

"She has a beautiful neck," Joe ventured.

"There are women in Pittsburgh," Claire said, "with gorgeous necks."

"The women here are all married or have boyfriends they should leave but don't. I've seen the statistics. The population here is old and married. All over Pennsylvania the young and attractive and intelligent are leaving for places like Seattle and San Francisco, where there's the possibility for natural catastrophe and more restaurants per capita."

"You're not twenty," Claire said. "The group that's leaving isn't your demographic group. Your group is the group that stays."

"I may be *old*," Joe said, "but I have a big heart."

"Is it big enough to fit a horse inside?" Claire asked, and recognized the commodity of not speaking English, the idea of not ruining things with language. Here, the Russian bride had an advantage.

"My heart is a great many things you don't know!" Joe said. He furled, unfurled himself in anger. He puffed himself up in defense and for a moment seemed to have plumage, wild and streaked and beautiful. She expected him, at any moment, to sound a mating call, shrill and unexpected.

"You'll never do this," she said, and it was her only bit of relief. "You never will."

"I'll do what I need to."

"You're crazy. Insane!"

"I'm lonely, Claire," he told her. "You don't have to rub it in."

Claire had hoped for not a woman but a Russian caricature, several crazed and angry and round versions of Elena stuffed inside one crazier and angrier and rounder version, all of which she'd line up like a set of nicely painted Matryoshka dolls. Claire wanted a madwoman with a babushka and an imposing set of hips, thighs that could crush Joe's graying head as easily as a walnut, but Elena had beautiful hair that, sensibly, she did not cover. Her hips were attractive childbearing hips, nothing imposing. She was an ordinary woman—no signs of madness to speak of—but Claire knew, in a pinch, she'd handle things. In a moment she'd become a woman twenty times the magnitude of the woman she appeared to be. Claire determined this from Elena's handshake, certainly not the flinty handshake of an imposter. In an emergency Elena would administer CPR, remembering to stabilize the body, open the air passage, check for breathing—things Claire had long ago forgotten or possibly had never known. She would construct makeshift splints, boil Russian remedies. She *handled* things: Giant Eagle on a Sunday afternoon, Joe's mother and friends, the rigor of daily English classes.

Claire had seen her English workbook, the paper cover still crisp, the assignments completed in meticulous print. The only thing it seemed Elena could not stand was the absence of her daughter, that sullen-faced thing whose photographs now hung on Joe's wall. But here she was, coming to America for the first time to see her mother marry an American, middle-aged and graying and not especially rich. Joe had planned a party for her arrival, a house party, an utterly inappropriate event, Claire thought, for a seventeen-year-old Russian girl making her way to America for the first time. She imagined Joe's friends coddling their Iron City cans, sneaking glances at the Russian daughter's breasts between hasty sips of beer. There would be, as always, meat and cheese trays ordered from Giant Eagle, too much Lynyrd Skynyrd, the residual scent of something damp and depressing in Joe's basement.

"Please," Claire said to Marcus as he shoveled the last of the snow into the street. "Go to the party."

"Sure, right," Marcus said.

"Please, Marcus." With the Russian daughter's arrival, this strange occasion, this wedding, was finally to be put in motion. She had, this morning at work, seen the dismantled layers of someone's five-tiered wedding cake strewn across the counter, and known it was true. She felt panicked by the idea that Marcus would not attend this Russian girl's party. It was not so much that she wanted Marcus to come as much as she feared, absolutely, attending alone.

At Joe's house the next night, a cardboard cutout of Jerome Bettis stood at the front door, greeting guests with a menacing expression, welcoming the Russian daughter to America with the hearty girth of his thighs, the formidable presence of his black and gold.

"Nice," Marcus said. "I'm sure this chick *loves* the Steelers."

"Everyone loves the Steelers," Claire said. As a gift, she had brought a bottle of wine wrapped inside a velvet bag. She felt self-conscious about this, setting the velvet bag next to the selection of liquors in plastic bottles that everyone else brought. It wasn't a party, she saw, where people were interested in varietals. Claire counted eight bottles of Vladimir Vodka, a cheap brand with a trashy label that was the running joke of the evening.

"Have some, why don't you?" someone asked in a fake Russian accent, nudging them toward a bottle. "Vladimir is the life of this party."

They discovered everyone huddled inside the kitchen like animals at the trough. The festivities, Claire saw, had not properly gotten underway; people hadn't drunk enough to know how to behave with one another. At the center of the crowd was Joe, leaning against the oven for support, his left arm clamped around a girl's bony shoulders. The thin girl cricked her neck to the ceiling. She stared at the bare white surface as if it provided a square of relief from everything unfolding around her.

"So fatherly!" Claire said without smoothing the sarcasm from her voice. She was noticing recently: like polio, her sarcasm could not be contained; really, it knew no bounds.

The daughter straightened to stare while Joe introduced them too loudly: "Marina, Claire! Claire, Marina!" He had, Claire noticed, the same affected voice her mother had when speaking to foreign people: loud and louder still, as if volume aided comprehension.

"Nice meeting you," Claire said. Standing before the Russian daughter she felt sedate, like the color beige personified. She had always thought the combining of various cat prints in a single outfit was a gigantic fashion *no*, but here was the Russian daughter, slouched before her and wearing leopard print as well as tiger print. She had wrapped something furry several times around her neck, and it looked poised and alive resting against her pale skin, on the thin verge of choking her. Marina flicked this furry thing away from her face as though for emphasis and stepped toward Marcus, simultaneously unbuttoning the top button of his coat and sipping from a bottle of bourbon.

"I *love* that," Marina said.

"Certainly," Marcus said, handing her the bottle. "Of course."

"She's seventeen," Claire said. "Right? You're seventeen. She's seventeen," she told Marcus.

Marcus ignored her; Joe shrugged.

"I've been to Moscow." Marcus sipped his bourbon.

"Really?" Marina asked.

"*Really,*" Marcus answered.

"I've read *Anna Karenina*," Claire said, and Marina stepped closer to Marcus, obliterating Claire from their conversation.

"Where's Elena?" Claire asked Joe.

"Somewhere," he said. "Maybe upstairs. She doesn't like these sorts of parties."

"I understand that," Claire said. She poured herself some Vladimir and asked, "Are you freaking out?"

"I'm a man," he said. "I don't freak out. I'm the epitome of calm."

"*Wonderful.*"

"I'm so calm I could, like, lead meditation."

"Great."

"Claire," he said drunkenly. "I'm about to be the father of a teen-age girl."

"Not really," Claire said.

"I want to be a good father, Claire. I want to do everything right. I want to encourage things but don't want to be too lenient. Do you know what I'm saying?"

"This is a ridiculous conversation," Claire said.

He shrugged, staring first into his Iron City and then at Claire. "What?"

"Can I touch your earlobe?"

"Please don't," she said.

He leaned closer to her. "I'd really like to touch your earlobe."

"You're really drunk," she said. "And freaky." She turned.

Outside, Joe's friends grilled in the snow. Iron Cities in hand, they joked about ordering their own brides, preferably skinnier, stupider, and larger busted, a conversation that halted effectively when Joe's mother stepped outside with the intention of getting a hamburger.

"Claire!" Joe's mother said. "Have you met Marina?"

"I really have," Claire said.

"Beautiful girl! I keep telling Joe, she could model!"

"She could escort," Claire said. Already, she felt drunk. She felt angry, contrary. She sipped her Vladimir intently.

"Joseph looks *happy*," Joe's mother said, ignoring her. "He went through a lot with that first divorce. I kept telling him, he's forty-four. He wants a family. He *needs* a family. They say there's a success rate with these marriages. They say these marriages work. People are committed in these marriages, dedicated to them. They all say this, and I believe them."

"Who, they?" Claire asked.

"The experts."

"I wouldn't know," Claire said. "I don't know anything about it."

"Arranged marriages worked," Joe's mother said. "In their time. People forget this."

"They did," Claire said. "Who needs something as superfluous as love?"

"For instance," Joe's mother said. She was looking intently at Claire's forehead, as though there was a mark on it. "Sometimes Joseph doesn't know what's right for him. He's too emotional. He might choose a partner who's too young, or someone who's already involved. He might choose a person who would really hurt him, someone who wouldn't care what he's been through. But Elena, she needs him. She's in a position to respect his feelings. She needs him to respect hers. That's a much safer place for him. Safety is an earnest concern, the older a person gets. Do you understand?"

"I do," Claire said. Looking down at her glass she saw, sadly, that it was empty. "I really do."

"Good, *good*," Joe's mother said. "*Good*."

Inside, Joe's band played a set. It was true: Joe did not have rhythm, he lacked all sense of it, but he appeared happy in his ignorance, banging away like someone lobotomized. The singer leaned heavily on the microphone stand. The bass player stared down at his moving fingers as if they mesmerized him.

"Claire," Marcus called during the set break, when Joe had finally left the improvised stage looking sweaty and disheveled. He waved to her from a dirty velvet couch, where he and Marina sat passing the bottle of bourbon between them, talking, talking. Sitting there, having sunk into the couch cushions, they looked short and squat, like sudden midgets.

"Ha, ha!" Claire laughed, nervously and too loudly, and Marcus and Marina stared momentarily away as if her laugh was the long, strange call of a lunatic they'd like politely to ignore.

"Are you finished talking, Cathy?" Claire finally asked. "Are you ready to leave?"

"Claire," Marcus said. "Have you met Marina? This is Marina. Marina, this is Claire."

"We met her," Claire said. "Together. You and I. Just a few hours ago."

"Oh." Marcus said, sipping bourbon. "Well."

"Ha, ha," Claire laughed.

Marina stared at Claire with what seemed a steely-eyed American glare.

"*Yes?*" Claire asked.

"I don't like you," Marina declared. She shrugged her thin shoulders. Her bare collarbones stood out sharply, like things that did not belong.

"We just met."

"So?"

"So, how do you know?"

"I know," Marina said.

"I don't like you." Claire landed heavily on the word *you*, emphasizing it, as if she were fourteen years old and believed herself capable of wounding people with italics. She suspected even Marina would shun this tactic, gleaned from the elementary schoolyard.

"Girls," Marcus said, waving his hand between them. "Girls."

Crossing the basement to leave, Claire could not help hearing Marina's laughter dissolving like very fine sugar behind her. "She doesn't like me," Marina was telling Marcus. "She doesn't like me, ha!"

"Your future stepdaughter," Claire told Joe the next morning, "is lovely."

"Thank you." Standing in his front door, staring out at the cold, he did not detect her sarcasm.

"I'm going to Giant Eagle. Do you want to come?"

"I can't." He peered into the darkness of his house. "There's dinner tonight, my wedding tomorrow." These words startled him; he looked momentarily askance.

"Right," Claire said. "That."

"I need to stay here. Be supportive, husband-like."

"Of course you do," Claire said. "You're getting married."

"Dinner's at six," he told her. "Don't forget—a Russian Feast. A traditional Russian dinner." He looked skeptical. "Come early if you want to."

She left for Giant Eagle still wearing pajamas and without having brushed her teeth or hair, the coffee in her mug sloshing when she took hard turns. She drove with the radio off, listening to the tires schlep, schlep against the wet pavement. At the store, she hazily gathered whatever happened to be in front of her: two bags of rice and beans, a family-sized box of Jimmy Dean sausage, frozen breakfast burritos the size of footballs. In line at the express checkout, a man sniggered at her pajamas and slippers, nudged the friend standing beside him, arms wrapped around several jars of condiments.

"Nice feet," man number one said. "Nice getup."

"*What?*" she asked. "What did you just say to me?" Her voice shot above the grocery store music, sharp and bright, like something rising suddenly out of mist. She chucked a breakfast burrito at the square of dirty linoleum near the man's feet, to emphasize her point. People shuffled their groceries to look at her; they took several careful steps away, and Claire suspected she should feel embarrassed, but she did not. She felt only pleased to have rediscovered her anger. Her anger had formerly been lost, gone astray like a confused pet. She felt happy now to have the entire express line focusing on it, giving it their constant drops of attention like something to be fed intravenously. She did not know when she would need this anger, but it comforted her that it was there, ready, eager, willing.

Marcus, pallid, did not feel like eating breakfast.

"I made it for you," Claire said.

"The thought of eating that makes me sick." He gestured toward a breakfast burrito, swollen before him.

They spent the day waiting, watching bad television. Marcus watched one woman's liposuction performed on a reality show. The surgeons flung aside this woman's fat as if flinging mud in a field; one held a lump to the camera, smiling, joking.

"Would you get plastic surgery?" Marcus asked, opening a can of Iron City. "Would you get, say, a tummy-tuck?"

"I'm not sure how to take that," Claire said. "I'm not sure what you're saying."

"It's conversation."

"Nice," Claire said. "Why this sudden need for conversation?"

"Did you know," Marcus said, "just five minutes of conversation every day helps build a couple's foundation?"

"Ha!" Claire said.

In the kitchen she assembled pastry swans while Marcus shoveled snow from the walk. Claire acknowledged his effort from the kitchen window with a sharp nod of her head. Assembling swans like she was, she would have preferred to be nicer, to provide a more fluid acknowledgement—a wave, a smile, something briefly undulating— but what occurred was the nod, quick and German, like something to be executed over barbed wire.

"See?" Marcus asked when he finally came inside. His knitted hat sat lopsided on his head, rose up like the tip of a condom. It gave him the appearance of being easily susceptible to things.

"What?"

"Things," Marcus said, "can be peaceful." He tapped the head of a pastry swan as if it were a pet dog.

"Peace, piecemeal," she said. "Dinner's at six."

"Right," he said. "Dinner."

In the living room at Joe's house, Joe set immediately into the platter of pastry swans, breaking several necks in the process, knocking them haphazardly on their sides.

"Joseph," Joe's mother said, nodding sharply to the crushed swan in his hand. "We haven't eaten dinner."

"I'm sorry." He held his uneaten swan in his wide palm like a pet he did not want to disturb. He wore, for the first time Claire had ever seen, a suit. It gave him the look of something stuffed, like a Thanksgiving turkey.

"Thanks for coming," Joe said.

"Of course," Claire said, but actually she would have preferred staying at home, ordering pizza, and watching television. God forbid Marina was here, sitting at the table with something furry and distracting around her neck, a maniacal, teenaged look in her eye. Claire imagined her, shoveling bites of meat inside her thin body and muttering between chews, *I don't dislike you. I hate you.* God forbid either she or Marcus drank too many swallows of whiskey. God forbid Claire drank too much Vladimir.

In the awkward beat of silence, Joe offered Marcus his pastry swan, delicately pushing it forward as though to protect its wings.

"No, thanks," Marcus said. "I don't eat sugar."

"Alcohol," Claire pointed out, "is sugar."

"Actually," Marcus said, "if you must know, the body metabolizes them differently."

Joe asked, "Would someone like a drink?"

Marcus raised his hand like a schoolboy. Claire noticed he looked shoddy and thrown together. His hair, atypically combed, looked like someone else's hair slid onto his head for convenience. He wore his only pair of adult-looking pants, the knees of which now had holes. He accepted his drink with an appreciative nod.

"You're getting married tomorrow," Marcus acknowledged.

Joe nodded.

"It's an important stage in a relationship," Marcus said. "The culmination of much hard work, striving to attain something significant." His voice held a thin ironic tension that Claire identified immediately. She concentrated on the floral pattern whirling its way across the couch.

"Sure," Joe said. "Of course."

"Is the language thing a hindrance?" Marcus asked. "Or is it a relief, to not always be talking, talking? Five minutes a day of good conversation can sustain a relationship. It's, like, a foundation."

"Really," Joe said.

"That five minutes," Claire said, "is either nothing or an eternity, depending on the circumstances."

"In my day," Joe's mother began, but stopped. From the kitchen the sound of yelling. The voices came, delayed, around the corners of the hallway: brusque, excited Russian like a sound clip from a foreign film. The four of them sat listening as if to the serious recitation of a poem. Joe's mother crossed and uncrossed her ankles. She, too, seemed to be studying the floral pattern on the couch.

Marcus, sipping his drink, asked Joe, "So what do those two have to fight about?"

"I don't know." Joe stared deep inside his own drink as one might look searchingly into a well.

"Seriously," Marcus said. "Come on."

"Me, probably. Probably it's a discussion about me."

"That." Marcus swallowed the last sip. "That, I understand."

In the dining room, Elena hovered over the table like a gnat, angling and reangling casserole dishes with a neuroticism Claire appreciated. She had put the fight with Marina emphatically behind her, directing her attention to the terra-cotta dishware, the silver serving

35

spoons casting her distorted reflection, but then Marina blew into the room like something hot to the touch, the end of a poker left to smolder. She wore a deep purple dress, viciously fringed. It appeared as if she might burst into a frenetic flamenco dance, impressing everyone with her flexibility. She pulled a chair from the table with a clatter, pulled a second chair out with a clatter. The dress shifted support around her breasts throughout like something with good structural integrity.

"This all looks very wonderful," Joe's mother said.

"It certainly does," Joe agreed.

A toast was made: to Joe and Elena. Glasses clinked confusedly, noisily.

"To love!" Marcus said, too loudly. Wine sloshed over the rim of his glass.

Elena nodded. Joe rearranged his tableware.

"Perhaps," Joe's mother said, eyeing Marcus. "Perhaps it's you two next."

"Perhaps!" Marcus said.

They settled into dinner with fierce determination.

Dinner, as far as Claire could tell, was meaty. Joe typically liked a meaty dinner—he liked meat, Claire knew—but in this situation, the meat shared too close a proximity with vegetables, and not the sexy Californian vegetables that one heard about, eaten seasonally and seasoned minimally. These were the lumpy, depressed vegetables of winter. Joe frantically flicked his fork, banished the cabbage to the side of the plate farthest from him. At the head of the table, his mother ate everything with an erect enthusiasm that declared: she was a woman with manners. She'd eat anything, given the need for propriety. Elena chewed carefully; Marina pushed her plate aside without touching it. The only person enjoying himself, it seemed, was Marcus, who steamrolled everything. Marcus loved food, and Claire loved this about Marcus. It was a selling point he had, like a car's having air conditioning or automatic steering. He loved, absolutely, to eat, to lean over his plate and declare that this food before him was the best, ever.

"Do you *like* Russian food?" Marcus asked Joe, nodding at the pile of cabbage on his plate.

"Not really. Yes. I don't know," Joe said. "We don't really eat it."

"What do you eat?"

"Normal food."

"Normal food!" Marcus said.

"My mother cooks for us."

Marcus said, "Your mother!"

"To make things easier on Elena," Joe said. "She's been very helpful, my mother."

"Your mother!" Marcus leaned across the table for second helpings.

"You sound so surprised," Joe's mother said, and Claire identified the forced good nature in her voice. "I'm a wonderful cook. I've cooked dinner every night for the last forty years. Ask Joseph. Forty-five years ago I went to the Sears cooking school and for forty-three years I cooked dinner every night for my husband. For my son, too, except for Texas, but we needn't talk about *that*."

"She has," Joe said. "You have, Mother."

"Sears has a cooking school?" Claire asked in an attempt to find steady ground. Things seemed to be shifting beneath her.

"They did," Joe's mother said. "A very good one."

"That's not the point," Marcus said.

"There isn't a point." Claire's voice was a warning flag. She was holding it out to Marcus as if to say, "It's dinner. There's never a point to dinner except celebration and enjoyment." She vigorously sipped her Vladimir. She sipped her wine. She could not help this constant nervous sipping. It felt like a signal before a storm, a tremble in the air and trees before an earthquake. She looked for John the dog to see if he, too, had noticed it—she'd read somewhere that animals supposedly noticed such things—but he appeared, unfortunately, more interested in the possibility of table scraps. He hovered at Marina's knees, draped with the fabric of her purple dress, which she nudged at him, urging him to leave.

"It's so American," Marcus said. "So insulting."

"Marcus," Claire said.

"What do you mean, American?" Joe's mother asked.

"I'm just saying," Marcus said, draining the last of his wine, "this whole thing is so fucking *American*. You all know what I'm saying. America. American."

"I don't, actually," Joe's mother said. "I just hear the same words repeatedly, *America, American,* but I have no idea what you're actually trying to say."

"Thank you, Marcus," Claire said, "for your *insight*."

"He makes a point," Joe said. To Marcus he said, "I accept your point. I've thought about this, actually, I have, and I accept your point."

"This is what I like about this man, your son," Marcus told Joe's mother. He leaned forward to address her specifically, and Claire sensed that she mentally shrank from him. "In his own weird way," Marcus said, "he's a good man. He might order a Russian bride, he might have that Pittsburgh provinciality, but he's honest. He had sex with Claire, you know, but he was honest about it. He told me about the situation, and it's hard to be honest about that stuff—*I slept with your girlfriend last week*. Although on another level you wonder why be honest with it. What's to be gained? It's something to think about, motivation. But on this point of the Russian bride, we can all agree: there's something unsavory about it. It's slightly off-center, it's weird, like the men who order those life-size dolls. It's like something we might hear about on a very trashy talk show. At any moment, there might be a brawl. Fists flying, oversized women yanking up their shirts to expose their chests, all kinds of pathetic insecurities. Anyway, in honor of the day, this momentous occasion, I propose a toast."

He stood up from the table, and in the process knocked his chair over with a clatter, which Marina reached to stand back up.

"Marcus," Claire said.

"A toast." He held up his glass. "Not to love, oh God, no, but to the abysmally fucking weird. To the abysmally fucking weird!" he said and, leaning across the table, clinked his glass against Joe's mother's glass: *clink*.

He left after this, like someone well versed in the act of leaving, like the husband who packed his duffel bag saying he was going to the gym for something as innocuous as cardiovascular exercise, and then. One minute his glass was clanking Joe's mother's glass, the next he was declaring that he needed air. Marina threw her napkin to the floor, followed after him. Claire understood she should be the one rushing after him with apologies and proclamations of love. This should be her, but she remained immobile, staring at her plate. Even the root vegetables appeared embarrassed, like they wanted to claw back under the earth. Joe's mother smoothed the napkin on her lap. Joe drank nervous sips of vodka and coughed. Spontaneously, he pulled his chair loudly from the table and went to Elena, landing a messy kiss on the crown of her head. He clutched her. "Excuse me," said Claire and went to the front door. She opened it and found no trace of either Marcus or Marina. The air Marcus had coveted was empty. She wanted to believe she saw their footprints patterning the lawn, but those could have been anyone's footprints, including her own. Across the street, the light in her and Marcus's apartment remained off. He had taken the car; this was disconcerting. She shut the door.

When she returned, Joe said, "Marcus took the dessert."

She saw it was true. The platter of swans; he had hijacked them. He'd left Claire without dessert, and this, Claire thought, was unforgivable. Her own transgressions were unforgivable.

"They were chocolate-filled," Claire said. "They didn't have that standard lame filling." After a moment, she continued, "That asshole."

Joe said, "Claire." Her name in his voice felt too large and itchy, swollen, like a bug bite.

She stared at him.

"I'm sorry," he said. "I should have told you."

"Told me what?"

"I told Marcus about *that*."

"Right," she said. "*That*." Her words had a hollow sound; she yearned to climb inside them and sleep.

39

Joe touched her shoulder. This was, she knew, his effort to comfort her, to be her friend.

"Don't you dare touch me," she said, turning. "Don't you dare."

At home, she called Marcus's cell phone. She called many times without receiving an answer, and when someone finally answered, it was a stranger's voice, a male voice, throaty, with the suggestion of something lingering, like a chest cold. It inspired Claire to reach for her own throat.

"Marcus?" she asked. "Is Marcus there?"

"Who?" In the background Claire heard a sudden sharp shriek, an incessant drumbeat.

"Marcus, the owner of the cell phone you're using."

"You have the wrong number," the voice said. "Marcus? There's no Marcus here."

"Marina didn't come home last night," Joe said, calling Claire very early the next morning. His voice contained notes of panic. Outside, it was just turning light. "Her mother is insane. She's screaming things I don't understand. Her mother is crazy. *My* mother is crazy. *I'm* crazy."

"Your mother is always crazy," Claire said. Her voice sounded dull, like it had been left too long in the ocean. She felt inexplicably unmoved by the situation. "Maybe they're at Sean's," she said. "He's usually at Sean's."

"Can you go there?" Joe asked, "and see? Please, Claire?"

"I don't *know* if she's there," Claire said.

"Please," Joe said. His voice caught. "It's pandemonium here."

Marcus's friend Sean still lived near the university, in a house on Ward Street catty-corner to a building that had nearly burnt to the ground two months before. Claire stood for a moment in the cold examining the cluttered porch: skateboards with the wheels shucked off, rusting bicycles, several crates filled with emptied beer cans, something that looked like a gas mask. Marcus had told her there were roaches that liked to live, in particular, in the dark internal spaces of Sean's VCR. There was a story about a rat that had climbed up through the plumbing and entered the house via the toilet, something about chasing it around with a broom. The front door wasn't locked. She turned the knob and walked inside the dim living room. Bodies lay around, rolled tightly inside blankets, like cocoons. She walked through the first floor, opening and closing doors, checking the faces of sleeping people. She was not especially quiet, not especially careful, and she suspected she should feel differently than how, in fact, she felt. She suspected she should feel on the verge of something, like she had been looking too long at yellow wallpaper—on the verge, maybe, of making a scene, garnering a reputation for ill behavior. She felt none of these things.

She found Marcus on a couch in an upstairs hallway, alone, a bath towel wrapped around his head so that the morning light would not disturb him. A second towel served as a short blanket. She jerked the first towel off his face. He shot upright, disoriented. Claire noticed blood on his collar. The left side of his chin looked prepared to swell. Immediately, he brought his hand to this side of his face.

"Where's Marina?"

"What?"

*"Marina."*

He sat blinking, adjusting to morning.

"The Russian girl. Last night. You took my pastry swans. Where is she?"

He didn't know; he had no idea.

"Is she *here*?"

This he did not know either.

"Can you *look* for her?"

"Claire."

"Marcus." Her voice carried little humor. He stood from the couch, the second towel wrapped around him like a skirt.

He said, "My head hurts."

She said, "I'm tired and impatient."

Sitting, waiting, she noticed Marcus had gotten blood on the couch; or possibly it was someone else's blood, but there it was, on the curve of the armrest, which he had likely been using as a pillow. She considered tracing the lines of the stain with her index finger. She thought she should feel angry at this situation, that the anger she felt in the grocery store should rise again like a thin veil of smoke, but she did not feel angry. She felt apathetic, scraped out like the insides of a pumpkin. She closed her eyes and imagined her own insides, those blush-pink organs, throbbing, the fleshy walls. She could have fallen asleep imagining herself housed in the pink room of her body, suffocating inside its lack of fluid oxygen, but there was Marcus's voice calling to her, sharp and hoarse: Claire. *Claire.*

Outside on the cluttered porch, Marina appeared, for the first time, subdued. Standing over an abandoned microwave, studying her reflection in its dark front window, she wore only the purple dress from the night before, rumpled and sitting skewed on her body like a poorly hung painting. There was, Claire noticed, a violet bruise the size of a thumbprint just beneath her collarbone, as if someone had pressed there, hoping to gain entry. In the daylight she looked her age: young. She fingered the bruise as though with hope of dissolving it. Her breath caught, unraveled, caught.

Claire asked Marcus, "Where's your shoe?"

He'd left Sean's house wearing only one shoe. On the other foot he wore a green-and-purple striped sock, which provided no exceptional barrier to the cold.

"What did you do with it?" she asked.

He stared at her.

"Right," Claire said impatiently. "Of course."

She kept a careful distance behind him as he made his way on the snow-covered sidewalk to the car, walking in his one shoe-clad foot and his one stocking foot. Progressing like this, hunched forward into the wind, he resembled someone much older, with greater pains and more complicated anxieties, an accumulation of slicing scars. When he stopped for a moment to lift his sock-covered foot from the snow, to warm it between his bare hands, it reminded her that, actually, they had once been young enough to think people could spend the duration, the entirety, of their lives together. They'd been young enough to believe it was possible, the faith to accomplish such a thing.

# MYTHS OF THE BODY

When Ana discovered the sex book, "Secret Lover" was on the sound system, a jazzy version, like something played in a water aerobics class. The book had been left on the toilet's ceramic lid like a sacrifice, an offering; still wearing her rubber gloves with their powdery residues of cleanser, Ana leaned the small of her back against the sink's basin and studied the various drawings. One showed a man and woman coupling, the man's buttocks disproportionate to the rest of his smallish body, each cheek looking as if it would soon birth some heaving monstrosity. Another showed a woman's reproductive organs, the ovaries appearing like rotted potatoes, the fallopian tube ending like a wire cut hastily during a crime. The uterus resembled a kinked pickle, something abandoned too long inside a picnic cooler, while, floating in the white nether-space of the following page, was a scrotum looking curiously like an apricot meant to be plucked and eaten. Written in that page's margin in an epileptic penmanship were the notes: *Sperm live inside the vagina for three days. Male pigs screw themselves into females' cervixes, literally. They ejaculate a pint. Their orgasm lasts a full half hour.*

Ana had discovered countless unfortunate things in the men's bathroom over the years, and this book, relative to those things, was no shocker. She'd found pornographic magazines with vaginas flapping in the open, emptied bottles of vodka, used and discarded condoms. Her most appalling discovery (simply because it wasn't as *literal* as the condoms) had been a pair of men's underpants wrapped around several stale hushpuppies. She'd donned rubber gloves on that occasion, called the district supervisor, spoken in her smoothest professional voice: *There's illicit behavior going on here.*

"Lucky pigs," Donny said when Ana showed her. She was frying fish that morning for the lunch rush, watching the fillets turn inside the burning oil as if to get comfortable. "Whenever I see pictures like that my insides feel like a trash receptacle, like someplace to put a cigarette butt."

"Women's insides are always nothing more than trash receptacles," Ana said. "You take things too personally."

"How else is there to take them?" Donny asked, pressing her weight against the oil vat's silver rim. On the sound system, the saxophone solo from Wham's "Careless Whisper" lilted through the dining room like it was trying to find an exit. It sounded especially shrill in moments, as if hurling itself against the windows in an act of desperation. Donny dangled the sex book over the oil with the perpetual deranged look that Ana had come to expect from her, slightly wild-eyed and hungry, the beautiful curved spaces beneath her eyes dark and angry, incriminating. She appeared in the simplest moments like a maelstrom, moody and bristling, looking as if her car had broken down on the highway and she'd hiked miles through sleet and snow and rain to get here. She looked this way now, as she ripped several pages from the sex book.

"Don't," Ana said while Donny dropped the pages with the authority of someone feeding an angry pet. They folded inside the oil like things attacked. "That's unsanitary. There's fish in there."

"The *fish*," Donny said, "is unsanitary."

Ana and Donny worked the morning shift together Mondays through Fridays. They had for months now, letting themselves in through the back door to the prep area, where they completed their daily mundane tasks, mixing coleslaw by hand in a giant sterilized garbage can, washing iceberg lettuce with a mysterious powder called Crisp and Fresh. They prepared green salads. They made pilaf, whisked lumps from the frying batter. They used to listen to the radio while they did these things, until the weekend cook lost his temper over a matter involving a late-night shrimp order and hurled the radio onto the floor. Now they listened to the dining room Muzak, upbeat instrumental versions of Whitney Houston and Celine Dion meant to placate the customers and remind them: yes, indeed, fish was innocuous *and* it was fun.

Ana had worked this job for a long time, since she was eighteen, straight out of high school. She was twenty-two now and had the scars from four years of hurtling oil to prove her service. She had started as a cashier, wearing a thin pinstriped shirt with an anchor insignia, a perky blue visor also with an anchor insignia. She rang up dollar-ninety-nine specials of fish and fries and two-piece chicken-and-slaw specials, always trying her best to *upsell, upsell, upsell!* The claims made in the restaurant reports were true: middle-aged men said *yes, absolutely*, adding pieces of fish and chicken, slices of pie, while their wives pursed their lipsticked lips, shook their heads *no, thank you.* Ana was an assistant manager now and had progressed to a more serious-looking polo shirt. Thankfully she no longer needed to wear any headwear, nor the apron secured with the giant safety pin one otherwise finds holding together a baby's diaper. These things, she knew, were progress. Her nametag was silver and engraved. This, too, was progress.

Donny had started only six months earlier, but her attitude was bad enough that she could have been around for years. She threw politeness aside as if it were a used carcass. "*Sir,*" she'd told the man who'd complained he had a fishbone lodged inside his throat. "*Sir, our fish doesn't have bones. It's all processed chop.*" To the man who complained the coffee was taking too long to brew, she'd said, "We're picking the beans in Columbia, sir, for your dining experience." She spoke in a way that made the customers turn away like small children who'd just farted in public or broken something glass and precious and had gotten their wrists slapped for it. Ana was supposed to reprimand her for such behavior, but recently she felt too tired. She was a manager but couldn't manage to manage. The weekend cooks batter-dipped and deep-fried cheap plastic toys from the vending machines when they were bored. They stuck the bright orange and red heads of the kids-meal troll dolls into the oil, the neon threads vanishing inside the foggy murk. They batter-dipped and deep-fried their own arms, seeing who could fry his arm the longest, and Ana ignored all of this with a newly perfected aloofness. They would never have done these things around Frank, who ruled with his fist with its strength of lard. He wrote up warnings, gave talkings-to in his serious manager's voice that had a tendency to sound British.

Lately, Ana yearned to pull the decorative fishing nets from the walls, sending their catches of carved faux fish with their bright beady eyes skittering across the floor, beneath booths and feet, underneath the condiment stand. Sometimes, when "My Heart Will Go On" came on for the third time in a day, she considered screaming loudly above the Muzak that Celine Dion was a whore. But unlike Donny, Ana was sensible, in control of her emotions. She addressed the customers with *yes* and *please* and *thank you*. She kept the permanent stitch of a smile ironed onto her face, like someone who had suffered nerve damage. This was customer service. This was her life.

Recently, though, Ana had acquired a stalker. She was living the sort of life in which having a stalker wasn't creepy. It meant things hadn't gotten too far out of hand. There was still hope for a person who could inspire a stalker. Ana's stalker had the kind of chiseled good looks she'd come to expect were off-limits to her. He was not daunted by the spontaneous buzzing noises sounding beside her, signaling that the fish or hushpuppies were done cooking. He was not made uncomfortable by the sharp pleats of her uniform pants, the residual undertones of malted vinegar on her skin. He was terrifically thin and pale, always wearing threadbare t-shirts and peg-legged jeans that emphasized the birdlike quality of his ankles. His hands, when he reached his money across the blue Formica, were attractively slender, capable of profound excavation, intricate maneuverings. For fun, Donny called him Hipster Jesus or, when she was feeling particularly venomous, Heroin-Chic Jesus. Ana supposed he did resemble Jesus in a dirty, severely cheekboned way. Not beatific breaking-bread-and-multiplying-fish Jesus, but risen-from-the-dead, zombie Jesus; Jesus-looks-curiously-like-Charles-Manson

Jesus. He came several times a week, staring at her with heavily lidded eyes suggesting he did not get much sleep, watching her while he ate his fish, and Ana felt singled out beneath his gaze, like the bright thing glinting in a dark rough.

He came the day of the sex book. The lunch rush had just ended. The scent of spilled vinegar permeated the air. "We Are the Champions" played on the sound system. In the dining room the remaining customers chewed their fish with pained expressions, as though none of them could comprehend it. Hipster Jesus had a friend with him on this occasion, a creature as pallid as himself, his hair sprawling upward like the tender roots of scallions. His jeans, like those of Hipster Jesus, sat extremely low on his hips, exposing sharp bones resembling handles. The friend blinked eyeliner-scrawled eyes. "I'd like a double cheeseburger."

"We have fish," Ana clarified.

"Oh, you have *fish?*" he asked, and Ana had the vague notion he mocked her. The song on the sound system transitioned into "Blame It on the Rain." Or was it "Girl, You Know It's True?" Ana fondled the coleslaw serving spoon's wide silver handle for comfort.

The friend nudged Hipster Jesus. "They have fish."

"We do," Ana said.

"Good!" the friend said. "I'd like something healthy."

"Nothing's healthy."

"Do you have vegetables?"

"Green beans."

"Organic?"

"Canned and gray."

"Is the fish fresh?"

"North Atlantic whitefish," Ana said, "flash-frozen at sea."

This went on for some time, the friend debating: two pieces of fish or three? Crispy breading or original batter? Fries or coleslaw? Hushpuppies? Would he like to add a piece, as Ana suggested? The line lengthened behind him, the customers shifting their weight, calculating the best deals as they stared at the menu board. Hipster Jesus forced his hands inside the tight pockets of his jeans in an attempt to locate money; his hipster friend wandered off to fill his Coke. As Hipster Jesus searched longingly inside his pocket, Ana did something she'd been contemplating a long while, something she'd been envisioning but hadn't yet mustered the courage to do. She scrawled her number on the back of a register receipt along with the brief question, *coffee*? Ana did not drink coffee. She did not have the personality for coffee, but it seemed a safe plan: no temptation had ever befallen two people having coffee midday, sitting on chairs so erect they threatened to shoot off like rocket ships into the atmosphere. Temptation could not befall two people sitting in a room of more serious people reading things like *Beowulf*, working crossword puzzles.

Ana tucked this paper beneath the lip of Hipster Jesus's styrofoam plate and nodded. He nodded back. This was an exchange sterile and efficient as the thinnest sliver of hospital needle, an exchange as subdued as a drug deal. It was done before Ana had the sense to stop it. And then she placed a handful of tartar sauce packets on his tray, despite his lack of enthusiasm for tartar sauce, and moved on to the next customer.

Frank pushed his way into the restaurant that afternoon, his shirt buttons fastened incorrectly so that the middle of him came together like a folded page, his tie twisted as if someone had tried hanging him but failed. He entered the restaurant like a mirage inside the humidity, his blond hair wisps of steam. The white streak of his part broke across his scalp as if to make way for something. For an instant Ana felt pleased to see him, like she'd just discovered five dollars in a forgotten pocket.

"Hello, Scranton store number 719!" Frank's voice was round with cheer and good intention, fattened up, a calf fed corn for slaughter. His lips puckered at the crown of Ana's head, and with this kiss he materialized before her, became flesh and body and bone.

Donny asked, "Did you know, Frank, that sperm live inside the vagina for nearly three days?"

"You'd be surprised how very *resilient* sperm are," Frank said in the same voice in which he often said, *This is very high quality fish, I can assure you*, whenever customers complained about the ambiguity of the term *North Atlantic whitefish*. It was not unlike the voice he used, inflated with importance, to announce the district supervisor's visit from Pittsburgh. Frank had nothing but esteem for the district supervisor. Probably Frank thought the district supervisor's sperm was heroic sperm, capable of living inside the nearest unsuspecting vagina for weeks, months, at a time, an entire decade. The district supervisor was due for his quarterly visit at the end of the month, and Frank had not stopped reminding everyone: the district supervisor was coming! He was coming! In a last-ditch effort to tighten ship before the man's arrival, Frank had ordered new training videos from Corporate. He had added an additional cleaning schedule for the brief lull between lunch and dinner rushes.

Now he ran his fingers through his tuft of blond hair until it crested like a perfect wave. He leaned against the ice machine in what he seemed to think was a jaunty manner. "Our coleslaw dressing hasn't come. It's wrong. I ordered it days ago. What are customers supposed to do, eat dry cabbage?"

"They'd choke," Donny said, voice plump with irony. "There'd be lawsuits."

"I might have to drive to the North Pocono store just to get some. And I really don't want to! Like I have nothing else to do! Also, we had six 800 calls, and five were bad. You figure out the percentage rate on that. One guy said, could we please clean the urine smell out of the side dining room. *What* urine smell?" He tugged nervously on his hair.

"Speaking of sanitation," Donny said. "Your incessant hair touching is unhygienic."

"Right, of course."

"Seriously, Frank. You wear a tie when you don't have to, you carry a *briefcase*, but you're constantly touching your hair and face, the most basic don'ts of any restaurant. Sanitation first!" she said as Frank leaned in to give Ana a second sloppy kiss, his mouth a missile that had lost course. She added, with what Ana saw was a tinge of disgust, or some other embedded emotion that made Ana

49

feel incriminated in bad behavior, "You two wacky kids. You two lovesick lovers. You probably went to high school together. You're probably, like, high school sweethearts. How darling. How *lovely*."

Ana certainly had never told Donny: she *had* attended high school with Frank, though she hadn't known him. Certainly, they had not been sweethearts. He was a year older but ended up in her tenth grade geometry class because he'd failed it the year before. He sat in the row across from her, one seat up, at an angle. While the teacher talked about right and acute angles, circumferences and axes, the girl sitting directly across from Ana and behind Frank had written things in felt-tip pen across the inviting space of Frank's neck: *Fuck Me, Masturbator, Big Pimping*. Frank had blond hair cut in a meticulous line beneath his ears, exposing his swath of neck, and Ana still remembers walking behind him in the hall and reading, printed there plain as day, *Cunt Magnet*. Occasionally Frank still reached to smear whatever might have been written on his neck into an incomprehensible blur. He still walked around like a man who'd never gotten over these things, as if he believed at any moment someone might sling raw egg at his face.

Ana had not been popular in high school, but unlike Frank, she'd had friends, a plump gaggle of girls who met on Saturday nights, baking brownies in the microwave and eating the entire lot of them, talking about how things would be better in college. After high school Ana had attended junior college because this was what everyone did who did not know what to do with their lives, whose parents could not afford four-year universities. She studied ceramics and made a series of heinous bowls with faux-leaf appliqués that her mother refrained from using for fear of lead poisoning. Her plump friends attended in-state colleges. They became anorexic, studied Early Childhood Education, drank beer from hats. They had sex with fraternity boys and constantly thought they had contracted chlamydia. Ana made several visits to these friends before realizing that they had moved forward in their jagged, haphazard ways and she had not. Her friends drank shots of Jägermeister and failed classes and had sex while she took long, rectangular pieces of frozen fish out of their boxes, breaking them along their perforations into proper fish-shaped pieces. Her high school friends did not understand when she explained to them: it was a difficult task, making fish resemble fish.

"Everything is so tedious," Ana told her mother over breakfast after she'd returned from one of these visits, the last she'd make. She was on the cusp of quitting school, though she had not known this. She was on the cusp of being promoted to management. The *Today* program blared on the television; Al Roker smiled cheerily over the weather. Ana's head had a leaden feeling suggesting it was not a head sitting atop her shoulders but a globe, an entire village of poverty that had located there, demanding water and rice.

"My God!" her mother said, sounding lackluster and metallic, like an empty soup can. "My little girl is grown up!"

Frank came to the restaurant two years after Ana started. She'd had to think to remember his name, but there he was, bumbling and inept, endearing to her in the plainness of his familiarity. He'd gone straight to management, shooting up the ranks with a ruthlessness that Ana didn't remember him having but that he'd probably gained from having *Pussy Licker* written in pink on his neck. He never put in time behind the register or as a cook, wearing his blue visor, fighting and fending off the hot oil. To this day, Frank did not actually know how to fry a piece of fish. Generally, the workers did not take him seriously when he tried to help with things, mucking them up as he did. They rolled their eyes at him, stood clear, and through Frank's ineptitude, Ana knew Frank was destined to be big management, a Supervisor. She saw the possibilities of their life together stretching before her like a paved and endless, frightening, path. They would have a house in Scranton with a side yard. They would one-stop shop at Wal-Mart for dependable white cotton underwear and life-long supplies of laundry soap. They would watch NASCAR, grill out, forget to have sex. They would have fat, insecure children who would inevitably learn that this was life. Someone somewhere had made these rules for living, and you simply followed them, salivating, waiting for the bell, trained in obedience, like Pavlov's dogs.

Ana knew: she still lived with her mother, who taught Ana her own inadvertent lessons about how to live. Her mother was having what Ana guessed was a midlife crisis. She spent her forty hours a week working as an administrative assistant before hitting the bars at night with her girlfriends, the lot of them wearing blouses and skirts a size too small. Her mother was, Ana thought, in denial about the amount of cellulite she had. In the morning Ana discovered one lone man or another sitting at the kitchen table, smoking, tapping the tabletop with his dirty fingernails while her mother scrambled eggs and fried bacon, confused herself with a coquette. These men had accumulated over time, referencing one another with their flannel shirts and stone-washed jeans until it became impossible for Ana to discern them: they were the rippling effects, a kaleidoscope of the same man.

"You're a slut," Ana told her mother the night of the sex book. They had, both of them, just finished work. They were sitting on the couch, eating Tastykakes for dinner. The television blinked its distracting images.

"Am I?" her mother asked, pretending to be displeased, but Ana knew she wanted to be a slut. In high school, Ana knew, you never wanted to be a slut, but after forty to be a slut was a compliment, like a rung of something achieved in Girl Scouts, more valuable than the sewing badge or the cooking badge.

"You should try it," her mother said. "Are you and Frank having sex?"

"God, Mother."

"Is Frank capable of having sex?"

"I forgot to mention," Ana said. "His penis got hacked off in a terrible accident, and now he's incapable."

"What I mean is sometimes he reminds me of a what-do-you-call-it, a eunuch. Do you get what I mean?"

"*Christ,* Mother," Ana said. She was trying to remember the last time she and Frank had actually had sex. She remembered it, vaguely, blurring into all the other times she'd had sex with Frank: perfunctorily, him moving her about the bed in such a way that she felt reduced to a sack of potatoes, a mass of snarled, rooted brown eyes staring up at him. Frank had sex the way he did most things: quietly, seeming somewhat dumbfounded, constantly touching himself and forgetting to wash his hands afterward.

"You know what I'm saying."

"No."

"Yes, Ana," her mother said. "You do."

Hipster Jesus did not call her. He did not even come into the restaurant, as if in giving him that single piece of paper, Ana had chased him away forever. She watched for him during the lunch rushes, searching the line of bored and frazzled people who frequented the restaurant, the mothers and children, the silent couples, the middle-aged men wearing the Hawaiian printed shirt and Bermuda shorts uniforms of summer. She stared across the top of her cash register into the dining room, at the bright blue booths with their flag insignias, at the wooden oars hanging on the paneled walls. The sound system played its steady rotation: "Sweet Caroline," "The Rhythm Is Going to Get You." She waited, waited.

The customers were difficult in the summer. They complained about the scant portion sizes, the sweltering dining room, the clam strips with their resilience of rubber bands. A woman called, claiming she'd ordered a ten-piece shrimp dinner very near closing time and had seen the cashier accidentally drop a shrimp onto the soapy floor being washed for closing, quite intentionally dry this shrimp on her filthy apron, and throw it in the box with the other shrimp. Even with the defiled shrimp, there had still only been nine shrimp in her dinner rather than ten. Also, the french fries had been cold, the coleslaw sour. For these transgressions, Ana wrote out a handful of gift certificates.

The employees, too, were restless. The heat and the stink of things reminded them they wanted more than this. They anticipated their brilliant futures. They snubbed their present shitty lives. They did things like drop shrimp onto the soapy, dirty floor and serve them to people. They forgot the fish in the vats and pulled it out of the fryer looking like burnt pieces of driftwood. They called off work for pulling a muscle while dancing too hard the night before, because their blood-iron level was frighteningly low, because their grandmother had died when she actually hadn't. They talked back to customers. They moped around and asked to go home early and ate fries out of the bin with their dirty hands in front of customers. They took prolonged smoking breaks. Donny, in particular, disappeared for minutes at a time during the lunch rush. She was there, dishing out Fish and More dinners, dropping shrimp into the vat, and then she was gone, leaving Ana to work the line on her own, to ring up the orders and dish them out and remember, simultaneously, to fry the fish and chicken and fries. Ana discovered her in the walk-in, simply standing there with her shirt off, the stark plainness of her bra, the sharp outline of her ribs exposed against the cool thrush of air. Several loose cabbages had rolled onto the floor like pale-green decapitated heads.

She studied Ana with an angry mercilessness. "I'm hot. This job sucks. I'm bored. I'm taking a moment to just deal, if you don't mind."

"Right," Ana said. "Okay."

Out front, waiting for Donny to return to work, Ana did not have time to lament the big things she might have otherwise lamented in the gaps between customers and fish: her lot in life, the choices she'd made or hadn't. She lamented, instead, that her coffee date with Hipster Jesus had not come to fruition. They had not shared meaningful conversation, pastry. He had not had the opportunity to treat her kindly and gingerly, as if she were a wound. Like a choose-your-own-adventure book, Ana had picked that potential path—possibly a good one—and it had not panned out. Instead she'd come to the end of the book to discover her protagonist had chiseled his way up an ice peak and died, panting from hypothermia, at the very top. The End.

She was surprised, then, when she left work several days later and discovered him standing in the parking lot, waiting—Ana knew—for *her*.

He leaned nonchalantly against the bright hood of a car, his pale skin exposed in the sunlight. Here, beyond the darkened interior of the restaurant, he appeared heroin-addicted, translucent, as if he'd been raised on skim milk and ragged vegetables. His hipbone nodded at Ana accusingly above the waist of his jeans, singling her out. Caught unprepared, Ana smelled of sweat and malted vinegar, cocktail sauce. She smelled like something expired. She had not—she counted—washed her hair in three long days. The pavement reflected the summer heat; Ana stood staring at it. The cook from the night before had spilled fish in rage across the asphalt on his way to the dumpster, and this fish was still scattered everywhere like an ominous sign, like locusts. Hipster Jesus stood now amongst the remnants of this mess, shifting his weight in the heat. His voice, when he finally spoke, was smooth, cool and collected as a throat lozenge. "I don't *like* coffee."

"You like tea?" Ana found herself resenting the fact that he was here, standing before her, having disregarded her attempt to make civilized plans. Beyond them, in the valley below, was the shopping mall, the Y in the JC Penney sign hanging unhinged and crooked.

"No, I don't like tea. I thought we'd hang out."

"It's short notice," Ana acknowledged.

"It's not like we're attending *prom*."

"True," Ana said. "Valid."

They stood for a moment, staring at one another.

"*I'll* drive," Hipster Jesus said abruptly, opening the door of the car he'd been leaning against. Stretching across the length of the front seats, he unlocked the passenger door for Ana. "Nice car, huh? '61 Corvair, only thirty thousand miles. I bought it from this old lady who drove it, like, ten times in thirty years. *Fuck* Ralph Nader. Unsafe at any speed, *right*? It's like, I can't decide: is the paint silver-blue, or is it blue-silver?"

Ana was thinking the situation already lacked the romance she'd imagined for it, her conjured romance. Sitting this close to Hipster Jesus, he had the dingy smell of last night's alcohol. He smelled like the interior of a Salvation Army store. Sweat pooled in the crevices of Ana's body. She was trying, subtly, to sniff her underarms. It occurred to her that Hipster Jesus did not know her name; it occurred to her that she did not know his. She stared across the parking lot while Hipster Jesus turned the ignition. The engine started with a temperamental huff. He drove through the restaurant's parking lot in a giant half circle, to the opposite side of the restaurant, the Arby's side, with its blinking cowboy-hat sign. There, he turned the ignition off.

"This car is a classic. You think I want to put mileage on it?" Something about his voice suggested he believed he was very witty. Ana understood he was not the person he thought he was. He was not the person she thought he was. The restaurant's gray wall loomed before them. They sat staring at it.

"My friend and I think it's funny," Hipster Jesus said, "that you're so young and, like, *manager* of this place."

"Assistant manager."

"Whatever."

"That's me," Ana said, "rushing up the corporate ladder."

"How does one get into it?"

"Into what?"

"The food service industry." He spoke these three words, *food service industry*, in a way that caused Ana to sit more upright.

"Actually," she said, "the fast food industry is one of the most stressful, after air traffic controller." This was something Frank had told her, tapping his pen for effect. He'd been very proud of this fact, loosening his tie as if in that particular moment he could no longer bear it, the stress was coming to a frantic, anxious head. "Our restaurant is one of the top ten busiest of its chain in the country." This, too, was something Frank had told her.

"Is it demeaning?'"

"What?"

"Well, is it?"

"Should it be?"

"I mean, you might as well strip for a living."

"That's logical."

"It'd be more *useful*."

Ana waited for Hipster Jesus to say something suggesting he'd been joking. She waited. The afternoon's humid ambiguity settled around them like a muff. Sweat rounded Ana's earlobe. In the distance, something resembling a buzz saw sounded. An air freshener dangled listlessly from the rearview mirror declaring, New Car Smell! People emerged from the restaurant, arms laden with to-go orders, most of which, Ana acknowledged, were probably missing some key component: the fish, the chicken, the utensils or tartar sauce. There would be phone calls, complaints, coupons distributed for free meals. Hipster Jesus was talking again, something complicated that Ana did not understand about his car's engine, the mechanisms of objects. He was talking about Ralph Nader again.

"My name is Ana," she said, interrupting him.

"Okay," he said, and she sensed his acute annoyance at having been interrupted. A brief and stony silence ensued in which they once again stared at the restaurant's gray wall.

What happened next surprised even Ana. She watched herself as if through a narrow slit. There she was, her, Ana, fumbling with the buttons on her manager's shirt, shaking it from her shoulders with no finesse whatsoever. Her skin appeared with a shock inside the sunlight, ripe with its residues of vinegar and grease, luminous. She was about to undo her bra, exposing her breasts as if they were pristine orbs. It would have been the first time, Ana acknowledged, they had ever seen the public, *dirty* light of day. She would have, but Hipster Jesus was asking, interrupting, "What the *fuck*?"

"I'm stripping. I've got nothing better to do."

Hipster Jesus's face appeared carved with shadows despite the day's unrelenting light. His voice swelled with complexity, with insecurity Ana had not previously sensed in him. She appreciated this, just as she appreciated seeing sports superstars cry: when they spoke of their mommas or attended church with their grandmothers, when they were arrested for accidentally shooting people and thus maiming them while visiting Las Vegas.

"People can *see* you."

"They're looking at the car," Ana said, her hand fondling then turning the car door's bright silver handle. Clasping her shirt around herself, she hesitated before leaving, long enough to say, "They're looking at this fucking car. *I'm* looking at this fucking car. Lord knows I've never had sex in a car like this. Pontiacs and Chevrolets, yes, but never in a car like this!"

And then, slamming the door hard, she ran.

"What were you thinking?" Donny asked when Ana told her this story the following morning. Ana did not know why, specifically, she told Donny, except that there she was, as always in the mornings, leaning against the prep table with a certain defiance, the line of her mouth drawn, her body alert and at attention—muscles, nerves, neurons. Ana sensed this was a story Donny could appreciate; it had themes she could applaud, a certain fuck-you quality. They were preparing shrimp together, lining the shrimp in neat rows across the paper-towel-lined trays, shrimp tails pricking their fingers angrily as if they, too, had found themselves insulted by Hipster Jesus and had only this singular defense. "Careless Whisper" was on the sound system again, the saxophone solo dipping into the song like a finger into jam.

"I wasn't," Ana said, "*thinking*. Clearly I had a breakdown of common sense, of rational thought."

"You should have done something assertive: let the air out of his tires, stolen his wallet. Dear," Donny said. "Darling." She placed a cool hand on Ana's forehead, and Ana fought the urge to fold into it, succumb. It was a gentler hand than Frank's: kinder, more benign. It occurred to her: she was not in love. She had never been in love. She was light years, in fact, from love.

"He doesn't love you, either," Donny said, taking her hand back, and Ana did not know how Donny had known that this of all things was what she'd been thinking.

"Of course he does."

"No," Donny said. "He doesn't."

"How do you know?"

Donny shrugged. "I just do."

They had lagged in their preparation of the shrimp. Outside, the regulars stood waiting for opening, their old lady scarves tightened around their heads like tourniquets, their old men's baseball jackets appearing polished in the sunlight. They squinted toward the sky, grimaced into the humidity, and for a moment, fumbling with the keys and unlocking the front door, Ana understood their finicky, deep-throated discontent. She understood their disenchantment. She did, she did.

That night, the single night of the week they spent together, when Frank entrusted the restaurant solely to the night assistant manager, Ana stole Frank's wallet. She stole it while he brushed his teeth with the same maddening precision with which he did most things, harboring it inside the purse he'd given her for Christmas with its fake leather like the worn, sun-drenched back of a seal, the same purse she never used but had carried tonight distinctly for the purpose of stealing Frank's wallet. She shuffled through its contents, wanting to find something incriminating and profound he'd been hoarding from her: phone sex receipts, photographs of his other girl-friend, large amounts of cash pilfered from the restaurant, a man's telephone number. *Wheel! Of! Fortune!* played on the television, the contestants grinning widely and spilling details of their lives: they collected their cats' fallen whiskers; they lived in the city but kept a yard full of geese. Ana found in Frank's wallet a punched-out card for a free Subway sandwich, a dollar bill, and several clipped-out coupons for various fast food restaurants. His driver's license showed his freckled face looking surprised against the backdrop, as if the person taking the photo had just screamed angrily at him to sit up straighter. She tucked his wallet inside her ugly purse and tucked the ugly purse beneath her arm like a pillow, waiting.

Frank misplaced nothing. Later that night, when he noticed his wallet missing, Ana suggested brightly, "Maybe you left it at work." He went methodically about the house, looking between the couch cushions, beneath the bed, for a moment craning his head inside the refrigerator as though he'd mistaken his wallet for lettuce and placed it inside the drawer marked *crisp*. He stumbled on from room to room, searching, and Ana watched him, waiting for some swell of emotion that might cause her to come clean, produce his wallet from her purse, profess her love for him. She studied him, waiting for a shocking revelation, but there was Frank, sitting despondently on the couch, looking as if he'd just plunked down a deposit for this chest, these calves and elbows, having borrowed them as he might have borrowed an inner tube at a public swimming pool.

"Are you okay?" Ana asked, leaning into him, testing him, burrowing the crown of her head into his neck, and he pushed her away, concentrating on the brusque turning of letters on the television, the implication of language, though his response was staccato: "I'm fine, fine."

"You're a strange girl," Donny acknowledged the next morning when Ana told her about the wallet. She was moody as usual, bristling, half-heartedly preparing the green beans and side salads. She was changing the sticker dates on the pilaf and coleslaw rather than preparing fresh batches, scraping the old stickers from the hotel pans vigorously with her thumbnail.

"What are you doing?" Ana asked.

"Working."

"I hate work," Ana admitted. "I hate it."

"Well, then," Donny said.

They spent the rest of the morning sitting on either end of the battered employee couch, watching the new training videos, amusing themselves with the stilted performances, eating pineapple cream cheese pie directly from the freezer. A woman covered her face with her hands, screaming, after oil flared into her eye. A man stood smoking over the oil vats while a giant red circle with a line slashed through it blinked onto the screen. A boy pocketing money from the cash register paused momentarily to glance at the camera with a look of decided fear. A worker lit a cigarette in the walk-in, hidden amongst boxes of cabbage. A group of employees stayed late after closing, drinking vodka and frying up batches of fish. For a moment Ana saw herself and Donny projected onto the television screen, their own example of a giant *Don't*: two girls caught in the couch's sagging center, their work clothes already inappropriately rumpled, an accumulation of empty pineapple cream cheese pie boxes on the ground beside them. This echoed the announcer's bleak sentiment earlier in the videotape: *Most theft, it is important to remember, is internal theft.*

"Did you know," Donny said, "the reason I came here? In Pittsburgh, I had an affair with my anthropology TA. My *married* anthropology TA—a beautiful, confused woman. Scorpio, talented, smart—*amazing*. She finished her program, got a job at the University of Scranton, and I followed her and her husband here, like some crazy person. Dropped out of school the end of my junior year. She's pregnant, actually. Due in October. We haven't seen each other in months, and I'm still here. Fucked up, huh?"

"No."

"Right," Donny shrugged. "It is what it is. It feels better than it did, and still bad. But better."

On the training video a worker running through the dining room slipped in a puddle of cocktail sauce. *Your caution and care now,* a voice intoned over an image of this girl sobbing, clutching her leg, *prohibits accidents and disasters that may strike later.* It occurred to Ana: it was eleven o'clock. The restaurant opened promptly at eleven thirty. They had not turned on the vats. They had not mixed the various batters.

On the television, a manager dabbed at the injured girl's leg with an ice packet, and Ana remembered grade school, feigning injury to get her hands on one such ice packet. She'd slit it open despite the warning, *Do Not Open,* simply because she'd wanted to know what was inside. She'd discovered blue oozing mush, which had been a disappointment. She'd wanted something more than blue ambiguity; she'd wanted a more specific mystery. She'd had no idea what to do with those blue insides once she had them, and this had seemed a great lesson about the nature of discovery: what did you do with it once you'd finally stumbled upon it? She felt on the cusp of making another such discovery, of slitting something open and staring down at its complicated mass of innards. She imagined herself sifting through these innards with bare hands that, like Frank, she would forget to wash afterward.

"We're late," she said. She was filled with reluctance that this was so.

"Things happen." Donny gave a vague nod toward the television. "Accidents strike."

*Rome,* Ana's mother frequently told her, sighing in her breathless way, *was not built in a day.* She said this at breakfast, at the kitchen table, while the strange man du jour flushed the toilet in the adjoining bathroom with uncanny aggression, as if annoyed he'd been coerced here in the first place. Typically her mother was wearing too few clothes when she said this, had darkened curves beneath her eyes, and Ana never knew whether her mother referenced her own life or Ana's, paying homage to the slow ways in which Ana's life accumulated, collected dust, refused to change. Her mother squinted over glasses of orange juice at Ana's manager's shirt, growing steadily threadbare, at the polyester workpants she'd been wearing since her days as a cashier. She seemed to be studying Ana's untrimmed hair, her flabby thighs, her tendency to let days stack up like spare pennies. In this particular case, Ana thought, Rome certainly was not built in a day, but the walls mounted like solid, indestructible things.

Donny had begun standing so very *near* to her, studying Ana with a curious expression, as if she'd contemplated the situation at hand and deemed her the solution to a long and complicated, sordid problem. Ana found herself constantly skirting around Donny, inadvertently knocking her hip to Donny's hip over the arranging of the side salads, the placing of a slight pile of carrots to the left, two yellowing tomatoes to the right, a bull's eye of cabbage dead center, just as the restaurant manual dictated. They hastily touched hip to elbow, elbow to waist, hand to occasional, accidental hand, and Ana considered ants passing in separate directions, touching their heads as if to convey something profound: the exact placement of a lump of sugar, a thirst-quenching drop of water. In this way, she and Donny communicated to one another. In this way, they began, though in the beginning it was very simple. They spent a great deal of time lounging on the employee couch before work, eating pineapple cream cheese pie, drinking the restaurant's watered-down coffee, procrastinating. It felt, Ana thought, *delicious*. That was the right word, a word Ana had never before used, had never felt comfortable using, a word reminding her of something plump and magnificent bursting on her tongue. It felt delicious to be so lazy, so haphazard, so careless, so urged on by Donny: *come on, one minute, sit here, relax.*

It was Donny who, having seen the video clip of the unruly workers drinking vodka in the restaurant past closing time, asked, why not? And Ana agreed, though not without acknowledging that in the following scene, the police showed up, jumping quickly out of their cars, raiding the improvised late-night party while the disobedient workers scurried to and fro like trapped rodents.

They waited until the last workers had left the restaurant, until Frank had left the restaurant, watching from a distant corner of the Arby's lot as Frank shifted his briefcase from hand to hand, dropped his keys several times on his way to his car.

When he had driven away, forgetting in his late-night stupor to turn his headlights on, they walked across the parking lot, unlocked the door with Ana's key, and punched in the alarm code. Inside they turned the sound system to a different dial, something that Donny preferred, raucous and loud, something Hipster Jesus might have played in his '61 Corvair with its mere thirty thousand miles, something even he might have swayed to in his peg-legged jeans. Taking their lead from the training video, they fried an entire case of fish for themselves simply because they could, just to do it, dipping each piece twice into the batter as the employee manual dictated. They fried this fish perfectly and even the district supervisor, Ana acknowledged, would be proud of their exemplary product, reminiscent of the photographs on the lighted menu board. They fried baskets of french fries and hushpuppies, and there was joy in such extravagant waste, for Ana pointed out to Donny that she had not had a raise since she'd been promoted to management.

"Is it demeaning?" Donny asked. "I mean, you might as well strip for a living. But anyway, as a consolation—" she held up a piece of fish as if to toast with it. "Most theft is internal. You're not, actually, alone."

They drank vodka, watched a terrible movie with teenaged '80s stars and uncomfortable one-liners on the VCR, pressed into each other on the narrow, battered employee couch. They awoke with a start to discover: they'd fallen asleep, paper boats of fried fish scattered about the floor, emptied soufflé cups of ketchup overturned. The television played static. The oil in the vats out front bubbled, hungry to be fed. They'd spent the night, sleeping in their crumpled clothing. In this morning stillness, the restaurant condoned bad behavior. The frozen fish and chicken waited silently in their boxes. The microwaves in the back room glistened bright and clean and untouched. The dining room's faux-leather booths loomed up like evacuated things. The restaurant urged them on, called them out: curve of stomach, arch of foot, thin hollow of neck. They rubbed against the neat language printed on boxes: *whisk slowly, USDA approved.*

Afterward they made a fresh pot of coffee and sat in a blue faux-leather booth. They watched the morning traffic on Route 6 slowly become more congested. The smiling fish sculptures nailed to the walls had knowing expressions. Everything smelled scrubbed and disinfected, clean. They took the time to fix everything they had destroyed, throwing away the extra fish and cups of condiments, tidying the employee office, remembering to eject the bad '80s video from the VCR.

They did this twice, three times, four times, five times. They lost count.

At home one night, before Ana left to meet Donny at the Arby's parking lot, Ana's mother eyed her curiously. "You're not," she said, "spending this much time with Frank."

"Possibly."

"Bullshit," her mother said. "That's bullshit."

\* \* \*

"Now listen," Frank said one afternoon at the end of her shift, calling Ana into the lounge. She sat on the employee couch, erect and proper, as if sitting too firmly on the cushions would spill out their contained secrets. "Something's wrong. The inventory reports are off. There's theft or there's waste. If it's theft, well, that's something. If it's waste, everyone needs to be careful about how much fish they're making, how much chicken. That starts with you, Ana. You set the example. I mean, something's seriously going on with the pineapple cream cheese pie. According to this we sell one piece of pie for every fifteen gone missing. That's crazy!"

"Insane," Ana agreed.

"Really!" Frank said.

The district supervisor was coming for his quarterly visit the following Wednesday. He'd stay through Friday, as he typically did, in the nicest hotel in Scranton, dressed in his pinstriped suits. He was desperate for Frank to figure out what, exactly, was up with the inventory this past month. Why was it so astronomically *off*? He had arranged to take Frank to breakfast on Thursday, and Ana knew from past experience that the district supervisor only did breakfast when things were in dire straits. These breakfasts always proceeded in the same way, according to Frank: the district supervisor ordered an egg-white omelet, out of concern for his cholesterol. He drank orange juice because the acid in coffee bothered his stomach. He took such lengthy pauses between sentences that Frank felt nervous he'd be fired in each ensuing sentence.

"The district supervisor is a simpleton," Ana told Frank in an attempt to console him.

"He's my boss," Frank said.

"You take that too seriously."

"I'm *your* boss," Frank said, getting up to take a customer complaint. Too agitated, he did not bother to kiss her.

It would be safer, Ana thought, for her and Donny to cool things off until the district supervisor had come and gone. Ana knew Frank would be constantly around during that man's visit, gnawing and nervous, pacing the length of the employee lounge. She meant to discuss this topic with Donny one early morning but was distracted, opening a box of pineapple cream cheese pie for them to eat with their diluted coffee. She ran her fingers along the neatly packaged slices, those endless triangles, and still did not believe the figures, one sold for every fifteen gone missing. It startled her, the things they were capable of.

When Frank discovered them that Wednesday, his key turning in the lock with a curious ka-chink, Ana felt not surprised but momentarily fearful of his reaction. She felt blessed to be so simultaneously old and childish, caught amid a veil of promiscuity and poor quality foodstuffs. In that moment she understood the reluctance of all things discovered, for here was their secret spread out for Frank to see, here was *it*: Donny's pale legs juxtaposed against Ana's tanned ones, their two bodies submerged inside the blanket Frank had once left inside Ana's car after the brief picnic they'd had. Donny's collar-bone craned as if reaching for something. Her hand briefly touched Ana's earlobe. Their skin appeared at once intimate and expansive. Frank's mouth, when he finally pushed through the lounge door unaware, groped for air. It made swimming motions.

"I'll wait until you're dressed," he said finally and stood outside until he deemed it safe to enter. When he returned, Ana feared he might gawk as if they were an exhibit at the zoo, two exotic animals who had thrown their scruples aside and mated before the blank stares of the kindergarten children. She expected condescension, possibly, or tears to be swept up like the fragile remnants of broken china. She expected anger, fire and brimstone talk about lesbianism, since Frank did, actually, still go to church. He believed, personally, that God was a smiter. God smote.

"You could have told me," he said, choosing his words very carefully. The only thing suggesting his nervousness was his toe, constantly tapping beneath the desk, keeping a steady rhythm. "I mean, I can't be with you, either. I have pains in weird places, some-times, over it. My teeth hurt. My gums hurt. We're very different! My mother and I discussed it. I was getting closer to doing the right thing and ending it, but I certainly didn't want to hurt you. You're a great person. Really," he added as an afterthought. He paused and stared at her. "But, like, you *fucked* me with the inventory, Ana."

"I'm sorry, Frank."

"I have to call the supervisor. You know that. You understand that."

"Of course," Ana said. "I understand that. *We* understand that."

"Good. Right," he said, and ushered them out of the lounge so that they would not hear his conversation. Frank had never performed well under pressure, under surveillance.

In the dining room, Ana and Donny slipped inside a front booth and waited. The traffic passed on Route 6. The fish sculptures stared down at them, steady, not appalled. Donny sat immediately beside Ana, paradoxical as she was: angular and pointy and at once rosy in the light, hair askew. She chewed the inside of her cheek hungrily, and her face was distorted, beautiful. Leaning forward, Ana traced her finger along the dark space beneath each of Donny's eyes.

"We're in trouble," Donny said, giving a bony shrug.

"Damn," Ana said and felt giddy. "Damn it."

She supposed that here, waiting for the district supervisor's arrival, they might have taken a moment to ready their explanations. They might have lined their lies between them neatly and geometrically, slipped to their knees and made penance, skinned animals, garnered blood. They might have shed heated tears, practiced the rhythmic chant of an apology. Waiting for Frank to return from his phone call, to plod back to them, Ana was certain she was not sorry. She was certain that even the district supervisor, amid the gravity of all this wasted fish, would not see the both complex and simple beauty of their actions. He would not have the capacity to discern: these were no wanton transgressions. This right here was discovery; this was what to do, and she and Donny simply braced themselves for what came next, what followed.

# BRETHREN

Jon prefers girls much too young for him; those of the tattooed-forearm and cat-eye-glassed variety; those who wear see-through vintage dresses and scuffed saddle shoes; who tote knitting bags in public and who lick their chapped lips nervously when they're talking to you. When I meet him at the café for the conversation he wants to have with me, he's leaning across the counter toward one such girl, saying no, her cappuccino is on him. His hand touches hers quickly, the way a gnat would alight on something.

He has, I've noticed, a peculiar pinched smile when dealing with the ladies, the disconcerting mouth-kink that other people have spent years of their lives trying to eradicate from their repertoire of nervous reactions. He's bowlegged and too thin. I've seen him walking down Grand Avenue with his curious gait, not unlike the wide squats my fiancée curses over during her exercise videos. He rolls the cuffs of his jeans to discomfiting heights; his shirts are the epitome of floral chaos—scattered, broken daisies lapse into elaborate embroidery at the shoulders. The word that comes to mind, when you look at him, is *honky-tonk*.

"Well, thanks," artistic girl number one says, and the ratty five dollar bill she's holding disappears, not into the tip jar, but her pocket. She's not as pretty head-on as in profile. She seems to know this; her head tacks steadily left. She sends a funny sidelong glance in my direction, gathers up her cappuccino and scone, and is gone.

"You wanted to talk," I say.

"You need a drink."

"A cappuccino," I say.

"No, no," he says. "This isn't that kind of conversation."

In the adjoining restaurant, in the hidden bar—I think technically it's called a New York or an East Coast bar, the implication being that we are not subversive on the West Coast but are obvious and unsophisticated, glaring—Jon pours us each a double shot of Johnnie Walker, Green Label. Here, the lighting is cool and shadowed, in the tradition of a saloon. Sitting where the bar makes its subtle curve, I half expect a large-breasted woman in western regalia to sidle beside me with a sharp, suggestive nod. Instead it's Jon, knocking my elbow with his glass when he lumbers onto his stool. We sit beneath the faint, flickering bulb that should have been changed days ago. This flickering reminds me of the faucet I asked him to fix weeks ago. During dinner service, drips accumulate, and I feel embarrassed. California is in the midst of a drought. Lawns cannot properly be watered. Toilets cannot frivolously be flushed. Tiny placards line the tables, demanding that guests request their own ice water.

He says, "I'm closing the restaurant on Sunday."

"What's up?" I ask. "A private party?"

From where I sit, I have a clear view of Jon's favorite painting, a vaguely Victorian and geometric lady floating on a black background, her violently red skirt forming a bell shape around her. She wears striped tights, has two skewed and squarish, unrelenting eyes. For some reason that I have never understood, Jon calls this lady Flossie, a name that calls to mind great aunts and their poodles. Flossie studies me from her floating position, and something in the shape of her eyes suggests she thinks I'm slow. She knows it. I use my fingers for simple mathematical calculations; I never remember my age, though I do know I was born in the month of February in the year 1972. I know that I'm a Pisces. A dreamer, the astrologists say. Jon is also Pisces, born in the month of February. Because of this, he says, we have kinship. We are born of the same blood; we understand one another. He carries his dreamy quality around easily, like the hipster messenger bag he uses and loves. When he stashes this bag

69

inside the restaurant's hole of a closet, he places it inside a larger, shoddier bag so his primary hipster bag won't get dirty. He has no use for a messenger bag. He doesn't ride a bicycle or a motorcycle. He drives a BMW SUV with a giant gash on the left side because he is incapable of steering in reverse. He conducts job interviews not by asking questions about wine knowledge and cooking techniques but by asking, *What is your favorite color?* And, *If you were stranded on a deserted island with only one food to eat, what would this food be?* This question is different than his perennial favorite, *If you could eat one last thing before dying a dismal death on a deserted island, what would this food be?* It means something to him that the food we settle for during the mundane rigors of daily life is not typically equivalent to the specialized food of predeath. It says something to him about the complicated—or simple—ways in which we settle.

"On Sunday, Sean, we're closing for good."

"Today is Thursday," I say.

"Yes, it is."

"That's four days." I have just counted on my hand.

He shrugs.

"That doesn't even get me to the other hand. That doesn't get me shit. You're telling me now, on Thursday, that you want to close this restaurant for good on Sunday. What you're saying is that I have exactly four days to find work before I'm screwed."

"Three, actually," he says. "We're not opening on Sunday." He has finished the last of his Johnnie Walker. He cricks his neck toward a high corner of the ceiling, preoccupied with the nest of cobwebs there. When he finally speaks, it's with the distant, practiced quality of a pageant girl answering the question she's just pulled from the glass jar. "Sean, you've been the best. Absolutely. And if I ever have reason to start another venture, if I ever need a chef for any reason, you will be the first person I call. Of course you will. Absolutely. *Absolutely.*"

Everyone in the restaurant has seen this coming from a mile away. From ten miles, twenty. A league. These days, customers are scant.

The servers, having little to do, flock together like dejected house-wives. They ignore what tables they have. These tables write deprecating online reviews. I've read them. They say things like, *Our server had such greasy hair you could fry an egg on it.* And, *My server seriously didn't know the difference between broccoli and cauliflower. That's taught in, like, Server School 101.* During dinner service, the servers pour vodka into water tumblers. They hide these tumblers behind the micros for quick sips. Glasses get broken, plates dropped. They giggle over these shattered things, mystified in their drunken states as to how to clean them. They poke their dirty fingers into the kitchen *mise*, steal shards of Parmesan cheese and candied walnuts. They order the wrong things and huddle around their various mistakes, demolishing them: a superfluous raspberry crisp, an endive salad that should have been made without the Point Reyes blue, an order of *frites* that should have been made without salt. In the kitchen, when it's slow, we clean things. I've made lists, items we can check off as we go: the bits of forgotten metal trim at the bases of the appliances, the accordion lining of the reach-in doors, the tiled backsplash with its vicious swirls of caked grease reminiscent of a Jackson Pollock painting. We, too, drink more than we should, but we clean as we go, and cleaning keeps us sober. It's hard when things are slow. It's hard when the end hovers like something noxious about you, beside you, getting itself tangled in your limbs and your hair.

My fiancée saw this coming. At home, sitting beside me on the couch, she mines me nightly for information, trying, every time, to be cool and cavalier as she works down her list of questions. *Were we busy? Did people like the food? Did people complain about the salt?* She has asked, *Will the restaurant close?* I say, *Yes, yes, yes, no, no,* and she asks, *Are you lying to me?* She has a sixth, eerie sense about things. I lie to her because, though lying is wrong, it has proven through the duration of time to be the easier option. She is high-strung and Scorpio, worried about money. We are getting married in October, and she likes expensive things she has no business liking. She has saved exactly thirteen hundred dollars for special chairs, fruitwood, with gold cushions she thinks will look better with the dark Brazilian wood paneling of our wedding room than the white plastic chairs the venue happily provides. *Fruitwood*, she describes to her mother with the lilt of a child's nursery rhyme. They spend hours dissecting the anatomies of bouquets and invitations, table settings. She makes stunning proclamations into the telephone, such as, "I can't have white plastic chairs in a room that is so dark and beautiful. I mean, I have an aesthetic."

"Chiavari chairs are gay," I've said, goading her. "The white plastic chairs are the bitter workhorses of the wedding world, and deserve as such to be respected."

"In that case—" She waved her hand, effectively dismissing me. "—I stand firmly against the proletariat."

I never would have proposed, but one night in the midst of chopping onions for dinner, she had paused and said, "If you were to give me an engagement ring, I wouldn't reject it." She dropped this statement into the ether, into the pile of paper skins on the cutting board. A less astute person would have mistaken this for a casual remark, an unimportant blip. I understood it was an ultimatum veiled as a casual remark, dressed up as though for Halloween. If the status quo we'd carved out through the years was to continue, it would involve a ring.

I had expected, when I went to pick out this ring, to find other wary, battle-scarred men standing, sharply exposed, against the jewelry cases' artificial lighting. I imagined that, surveying the landscape of solitaire and marquis and square-cut diamonds, we might nod to one another in much the same manner that Harley riders exchange aloof waves while passing on the road. We were, together, part of an elaborate network of men vying for our futures, and for something indiscernible. I imagined men, larger and less confident than even I, turning dainty rings in their oversized hands, maybe slipping them seductively onto their pinkies.

"The average budget—" the saleswoman began; her name tag declared she was Olga, and she appeared to want to tuck me beneath her arm like a little dove, to smooth my ruffled feathers. "—the average budget a man considers when purchasing an engagement ring is two months' salary."

"Are you kidding?" I asked, but Olga did not kid. She stared at me across a display of diamond pendants with the expression I imagined people had when they'd accidentally swallowed a bit of their own vomit. I had the strangest desire—*need*—right then, for Olga to lean across the immaculate glass countertop and slap my cheek. She simply brushed something invisible from her jacket, and together we went about the business of choosing a ring.

Later, I felt bad that I had not managed something better for the proposal. I hadn't booked a carriage drawn by dirty white horses. I hadn't reserved a fancy dinner, tucking the ring inside an appetizer, something she might accidentally choke on, spurring an anecdote we might tell people at dinner parties about our *amuse-bouche*. I had not found a picturesque fountain, or a park bench. I had not produced a scavenger hunt with little clues composed of our favorite catch phrases, our favorite haunts, our history together, the public places we'd had sex. My proposal, impromptu, took place on the couch, in front of the television. The ring, which I'd picked up that day from the store, had already burned a metaphoric hole in my pocket. There was not any view to speak of, save the brush rising thickly in the television background, while in the foreground a man whose hands and feet literally resembled tree limbs stared into the distance, evaluating it, as his cousin bathed him with a ratty sponge. I slid the ring on Vi's finger, and something tugged inside of me, insinuating that I had failed miserably and that this, here, was merely the beginning of countless failures that I would make.

Alternating her attention between the ring and the television screen, Vi said, "I like that you added elements of the grotesque to this proposal." Her kiss landed against my cheek.

"Ha," I think I said, but could not have said that I knew what she was talking about.

Friday night, she comes into the restaurant for dinner. This is something she never does, but now, with the end nigh, she deigns to do.

She works in fine dining, in a restaurant where everything but the food itself is whisked to the table on napkin-lined trays; a restaurant where a fork carried to the table in a waiter's bare hand has the same incongruity as a beach ball hurtling through outer space. She places Caesar salad on the table with the rounded tops of the leaves facing away from the guest; she sets slices of pie with their points pointing toward guests' hearts like daggers. She arranges braised meats to face them like upturned mouths. Guests cannot be directed to the restroom. They must be walked there, gingerly, and the napkins they've abandoned in crumpled heaps on their seats must be swept up, folded.

At work, my fiancée wears a starched button-down shirt and a serious, sour-mouthed expression. She speaks in a low voice that's not practical for the sort of people who eat at her restaurant. The clientele is geriatric, the sort who, having a tenuous grasp on their minds, ask, "Are you the woman with the hat?" to the bald waiter with the raspy voice. At work, my fiancée is continually dodging canes and walkers, the occasional oxygen tank. Tableside, she refuses to say *you guys*. She says *you two, you three, you four*, capping the expression at *you five*; the word *folks* makes her cringe. The old people love her, call her adorable. She's a cute girl, it's true, not beautiful, and early in our relationship I told her so, thinking she was reasonable enough to hear it, thinking it was something I could confide in her. I thought, mistakenly, that we were capable of even the difficult conversations. It still pains her; occasionally, she'll say in a stilted voice, "I don't know the answer to that, Sean. Maybe if I were beautiful I'd know the answer to that."

She sits at the kitchen counter, her wedding magazine spread before her. She mulls over an article about wedding-day lingerie, chews her cheek as if it's an ear of corn. The magazine's bold caption barks out something about tummy minimizers. I stare at her through the dividing glass that seems not to have been spot cleaned in days. She wears a vintage sundress à la artistic girl number two; the collar is a bow tie that's cinched around her white neck, giving her the faintest suggestion of an ostrich. Her hair has a messy, slept-in look. Paired with the vintage, ostrich-plumed dress, so pretty that strangers passing on the street compliment her on it, is the ugly red tote she received as a gift for registering at Macy's. It hangs from her chair like a sac filled with blood, like something carted around in the back of an ambulance in case of emergency. She is full of contradictions that come at me daily at an alarming rate. It's hard to keep up with these contradictions, as though she is the advanced level of a video game that I've failed to master. She wears pretty dresses but can't accessorize. She likes gardening but watches football. She reads feminist theory but drinks up glossy magazines chastising women for their dimpled thighs and drooping upper arms. She believes herself to be generous but has no idea how acutely she insults things. She notes flaws with precision; nothing quite measures up. Normally she would say, *This wine is flabby.* She would say, *This meager bun can't support the heft of that burger.* She would say, *This tenderloin is a touch dry.* She would comment on the amount of salt I've used.

Damian approaches with his order pad, and soon they are discussing the evils of New American Oak, something I suspect Damian knows nothing about, but he is gay and therefore a good liar. I suspect he has lied to me about customers' reactions to my food. "They love it," he says, but both the tension in his voice and the intricate working of his nostrils tell me otherwise. I have developed the bad habit of staring across the dining room, watching people take their first bites of steak, pork chops, tartare. I want to learn something from these bites, but the online reviews say things like, *The kitchen staff here is creepy, lecherous. If you're not careful, you might find yourself dismembered in the trunk of one of their cars.*

Damian eyes my fiancée with approval; she's turned on the charm for him. Unlike me, she exudes charisma. Her job trains her in the art of paving over her emotions, reducing them to nothing more than chronic good cheer, the equivalent of low-grade happiness. Sometimes if customers say condescending things to her, she writes *fuck you* on the white notepad beside their orders. She writes things like *fat bitch,* but to their faces she smiles and nods. She might hate you, but you'd never know it. She remembers details: when your birthday is; your anniversary; how many children you have; which one plays the trombone; which one received a scholarship; where you proposed; where you live; whether you take extra pepper or you don't; whether you have a problem with sodium or can't digest gluten; whether you are allergic to shellfish, garlic, or peanuts; whether you like the Niners or the Raiders. And on and on and on; it's dizzying.

If I hate you, you'll know it. If I think you're an idiot, you'll know it.

"No, no." Damian taps his fat thumb on a particular bra. "That's far too plain. Certainly not glamorous enough for the wedding day. That underwear is the gateway to nothing except disappointment and boredom."

My fiancée chews the inside of her cheek, contorting her face into something momentarily grotesque. I think of myself saying, "You're a cute girl, but not beautiful." I've seen this expression before; she's preparing to make the transition into what she really wants to talk about. She's examining the least circuitous route to the exact place, trimming away the superfluities. "How do you feel," she says, "about the restaurant's closing?"

"That." Damian gives a wave. "We saw that coming from a mile away."

"I guess so," my fiancée says, and though my head is down, avoiding her, I feel her looking intently in my direction.

"The thing that sucks is this whole getting paid under the table thing. You know, no unemployment."

"I guess not," my fiancée says.

She doesn't have dessert. I feel relieved; our desserts are never good. One of the girls from the adjoining café makes them whenever she feels like it. They are often fruit concoctions created with canned fruit and no expertise. The fruit overcooks, while the crisp topping comes out underdone. Her flan curdles. Her crème brûlée comes out soupy. Her crust tastes too heavily of shortening. Jon, on the rare occasions he's present and accounted for, huddles in a corner of the kitchen, eating these desserts ravenously. It makes me nervous to hear how much he likes these things, and to hear how much he likes my own food. He stands in a back corner of the kitchen, in the way of the dishwasher, eating with his mouth open, saying he'd love to marry me in between gluttonous bites of the dinner specials. It worries me that the only person who thinks I do good work is an idiot.

My fiancée's kiss goodbye, given awkwardly over the counter, is perfunctory, a kiss that conveys the sharpened, acute message that most words fail at. On her way out, she is intersected by Damian, who hugs her, pressing her ostrich neck against his own tanned fat one, telling her to come back soon.

"But oh, wait, you can't," he says with a shrug, and then she is gone.

"I like the way you work," a man comes up to the counter to tell me. "I like the way you run a kitchen." He's heard we're closing; Damian told him as he served his coffee, accidentally spilling the liquid onto the saucer so that he was forced to pour a new one. I watched this messy business from afar, lamenting all the things we've done wrong, that we've never once done right. All the things we'll never have the opportunity to do right, to make right.

"You make some funny expressions when you chop things," his wife says.

"You sure as hell do," the husband says, and together they smile and walk out the door forever.

"Tweaker," Jack working in pantry says, vigorously whisking the dressing in its container.

"Here's the thing," my fiancée said when she realized the extent of the things I did, all things she'd never done in her life. Occasionally, maybe, she'd mixed some peach schnapps and orange juice from her parents' bar, but she'd never once smoked a cigarette. She'd never done drugs. It was early in our relationship. I'd been doing a lot of speed with a chick named Maya we both worked with, a big girl with a fondness for the word *cunt*, as well as the hazelnut gelato, which on several occasions she'd eaten straight out of the counter with a saliva-dribbling intensity that made me look away, as though I'd just seen her naked. She got into some trouble, later on, for identity fraud, and I could understand why she'd rather be someone else.

"Here's the thing," Vi said. "I don't spend time in relationships with people who use a lot of drugs. So even though I'm not beautiful, I'm only cute, if you want to be with me you're going to have to make a few hard decisions about that."

On this particular occasion she had an assured firmness that made her beautiful, though I couldn't tell her so; it was a tender subject. She stood beside me, so close I could see the scar from her biking accident marring her lip, her unibrow, her forehead that took up half the space of a normal forehead, her cheeks that were not rouged, only wind-chapped, and I did not tell her she was beautiful, because I was frightened to. On this particular occasion, I drew her close and kissed her, kissed her, kissed her.

I grill steaks for our staff dinner, to run them out. If nothing else, we will eat like kings and queens tonight on Jon's dime. We'll eat the steak and the pork tenderloin, the halibut and the prawns, what remains of the vegetables growing limp inside the walk-in's stale air. Vi would dismiss this feast because none of it is precious and organic and a man with dirt lodged underneath his fingernails isn't selling it at the Saturday farmers' market. Jon doesn't buy food from vendors, and he certainly doesn't buy it from farmers. He makes last-minute runs to the awful bulk grocery for what we need. The store is called Jetro Cash and Carry, but he'll say, joking, "I'm running down to Ghettro." He wanders into the restaurant at 8 p.m. with the ingredients I asked to have by noon. He once sent his teenaged daughter into the restaurant in the middle of dinner service, hugging a saran-wrapped lamb shoulder to her pink Abercrombie-clad chest. She dragged the thing through the dining room with a slow step and slide, step and slide, like a wounded man dragging his dead leg behind him.

"You wanted meat," she said, speaking in the feigned chipper voice in which she always spoke and that I found disconcerting in someone her age. I saw, looking at the lamb shoulder encased in its plastic cocoon, that Jon hadn't had the courage to deliver it himself.

I hadn't asked for lamb shoulder. I'd asked for rack of lamb. I'd asked for it the day before. Jetro Cash and Carry most likely had a special on lamb shoulder, its price emblazoned on an orange flag stuck into the center of it, and on a whim he'd tossed it into the cart, arguing with himself that an animal's body parts were an animal's body parts, interchangeable. Jon is the person that supermarkets develop elaborate displays for, the prototypical sucker the men in suits discuss at their weekly meetings. I imagine they circulate photocopies of his blank face around the conference table, that he is the single reason they stock whipped cream and packaged shortcake suggestively beside the berries, the reason they stock fancy tongs next to the packages of ground beef. He wanders through the aisles, picking things up, putting them down again, going back to retrieve them, forgetting where his cart is, taking someone else's, never realizing that the box of tampons and five cans of aerosol hairspray are not his own. He's the epitome of confusion. You'd think a man who owns a restaurant would at least know his cuts of meat, but Jon buys flat iron steak when I ask for rib eye, pork chops when I ask for pork tenderloin. He has no idea, no matter how many times I explain it to him, what pork butt is. He could give two shits about organic, sustainable. He buys corn fed rather than grass fed, chicken pumped full of antibiotics. Omega-3 eggs are, to him, something from a science fiction movie. My fiancée shudders at all of it. She spends hours at the farmers' market, wrapping her hands around tomatoes with the same open-mouthed intensity of a man touching a woman's bare breasts.

One of the servers has heard a rumor: another restaurant is moving into this space by the end of the month. It seems impossible to me that this could already be happening, but looking for *cooks wanted* ads on Craigslist, I see it. The chef claims to want cooks who know who Richard Olney is, cooks who are well traveled and well read, cooks who want to make delicious food and who want at the same time to wait the tables and wash the dishes and banish forever the dichotomy between front of the house and back of the house. At the end of every sentence rings an implied *man*. I want cooks who know who Richard Olney is, *man*. I want cooks who want to make delicious food and banish the dichotomy, *man*.

"How's he banishing shit," my fiancée wants to know, "if he's only asking for cooks to apply? See, *looking for cooks*." She leans over my shoulder, investigating the ad. Her breath has a certain morning milkiness to it. She also smells of toast. "Also, a man who uses words like banish and dichotomy in the same sentence should understand correct apostrophe usage. You haven't earned the right to banish anything if you don't know the difference between its and it's."

"I love Richard Olney," I say, practicing. "He's my hero."

"I like to have serious philosophical discussions about his profound ideas while simultaneously chopping mirepoix and infusing oil," my fiancée says, mocking me. "In fact, just last week I had sex with his wife." She says, "You have no idea who he is."

"I'll Google him, Wikipedia him. I'll start a Facebook fan group in his honor."

"He was a food and wine writer." Her voice has an edge, like I've just forgotten her birthday or the fact that we're engaged.

"All right," I say.

"What this means is that Jon has known for a long time, a lot longer than four days, that the restaurant is going to close. He's known for a long time but chose to wait until four days beforehand to tell you because he lacked the balls."

"Yeah, well," I say, distracted by her use of the word *balls* to mean something other than what you'd find in a gymnasium. "You don't kick a man when he's down. He's lost his restaurant, and probably he'll lose his house. He has kids."

"When a man's a motherfucker," she says, "you kick him where he needs to be kicked." She makes a motion with her leg, simulating the supposed kicking of an asshole in his balls. This action causes her to remember. "I'm not happy with you," she says. Her leg falls slack. "When were you planning on telling me about the paychecks? The unemployment? All of it?"

"Probably never," I say.

She sits staring at me. I feel, suddenly, like a complicated riddle.
"You terrify me," I say. "You aren't always reasonable."
"I'm as reasonable as you inspire me to be," she says.
"Oh," I say.
"Yeah, oh," she says.

When the restaurant first opened, Jon hooked up with one of the bussers. She was exactly half his age, the insecure, crazy type that throws glass objects against concrete ones in intense fits of anger; the sort that always has the residual, post-cry stains of mascara inking her face like an emotional hieroglyphics. They took long weekend trips to Santa Cruz when he should have been perfecting the wine list, chatting up customers, studying the diagram of the cow pinned to the bulletin board. They swept into the restaurant at the end of these trips battle scarred, bruise-kneed, zinc slathered onto their sunburnt noses. Jon developed the bad habit of wearing pineapple-printed Aloha shirts unbuttoned at least three buttons beyond most peoples' comfort levels; of clasping the busser girl's waist as if it were something buoyant on the ocean that might save him from drowning. They kissed messily and publicly over their table's tealight, threatening to catch themselves on fire, intermittently eating french fries and pawing at one another with oil-stained hands. They behaved like two people who had recently discovered the sheer novelty, the flexibility, of their tongues. This liaison ended abruptly after a number of incidents: one broken toe while surfing, ten smashed votives, two absent menstrual cycles. Several times after declaring the relationship over, the busser girl came back , too young to have learned that essential lesson: for true dramatic effect, you leave when you say you're leaving.

I saw Jon's ex-wife once, briefly, when he and I went to the farmers' market one Saturday afternoon in the hope of incorporating more seasonal produce in the menu. A woman emerged screaming from behind a display of artichokes; she held one in her right hand as if it were a grenade she wanted to fling in Jon's face, exploding it to nasty burnt bits.

"Jon, you piece of shit! You fucking asshole! You dirty piece of shit!" In the background, a reggae band played happily. Jon's two teenaged daughters hovered, shivery and nervous, beside a collection of eggplant. Never relinquishing her grip on the artichoke, the ex-wife launched into a tirade, a litany of things he'd failed to do, had never done, would never do. He stood with his hands pressed deep into the pockets of his Bermuda shorts, sliding the toe of his Tevas back and forth in a dusty patch, drawing a line between him and the ex-wife. When she'd finished, he asked simply, "Are you done now?" sounding like a defeated student asking his leave from Sister Mary Catherine, who'd just slapped him across the knuckles with a ruler. The daughters focused intently on the eggplant, lifting pieces of it up like hand weights. The older one completed several biceps curls.

"Those shoes," the ex-wife said. "That shirt. Must you show the entire planet your chest hair?"

"Crazy ex-wife bitch," Jon said, watching as she pushed her way through the throng of vegetable-shoppers, away from him. The daughters scurried after her without even a vague wave in his direction. Afterward, we went through the motions of studying produce.

"I don't know," Jon said, lifting up a beautiful red bell pepper. "I think I'd rather just have a drink. Do you want a drink?"

In the bar, staring down at his Johnnie Walker, he said, "I only ever wanted to do very good by her." Uncomfortable with the gravity of this subject, he transitioned into another subject entirely. "You know, Jeanine is totally willing to still give me blow jobs. I guess it's the advantage when they're young like that, and really insecure. You want another one?" Flagging down the bartender, he ordered us another round.

Jon tells us that he'll show for the restaurant's last night, but seven o'clock comes and there's no sign of him. Eight o'clock comes, and nine o'clock. A woman sitting at the kitchen counter has been waiting for him since six. She's his age, a hard-faced, average-looking woman who compensates by accessorizing. Occasionally she reaches a hand deep inside her oversized bag, swirling it inside the thing's leather innards, fishing around, and each time bringing the hand up empty. She cranes her neck, watching for Jon's sudden appearance.

"Do you know where he is?" she asks me, and there is lipstick smudging her front tooth. "We're supposed to meet. Doesn't he need to oversee something? Isn't he the boss?"

"He hasn't overseen anything," I say, "since he opened this place."

"Oh," she says.

The next thing I know, we're closed for good, the few customers we had have left, and even the woman waiting for Jon has abandoned her post and gone on to better things. Thumb-printed glassware has collected on the various tables and counters, window ledges. The air has a certain thick smokiness. At least thirty people I've never met before, friends of the waiters and bartenders, have heard that Jon's not here; they've shown up to suck down the rest of the liquor. I'm taking it all in, waiting for someone to pour me a shot of bourbon, when Damian, already a little drunk, sidles too close beside me.

"Do you want to know a secret?" he asks.

"Sure." I take a step away from him. "I want to know a secret."

"Jon wanted to fire you. He talked a bunch of shit about you all the time. Behind your back. He talked a lot of shit."

"Why are you telling me this?" Something inside me feels hollow and wrong.

"To your face, though, he was something different. That's Jon. He's an asshole. I thought you should know."

"Yeah, well," I say. "What does it matter?"

"I guess it doesn't," Damian says.

"The only person I care about how he acts," I say, "is myself."

"That's noble," Damian says with a shrug.

The next time I see him, he's drunk enough to have stripped down to his underwear. He prances through the dining room wearing a pair of tighty whities, performing pirouettes between tables. A group of girls huddles in the dish pit snorting cocaine from one of the butcher blocks. Between them, they're wearing a great many silken scarves, appliqued flowers, and patterned tights. They're talking about someone coming on to them, and I realize after a few moments they're talking about Jon. A blond girl with a deathly pallor, as if she's just seen someone's severed body part, says, "He grabbed my ass, you know, as though he thought I'd like it. His wife was in the next room. And his kids. I was like no, thank you, and he went in to try to kiss me."

In the dining room, tables and chairs are curiously overturned. Natasha, a server who's never placed a single order correctly in her life, holds a giant glass serving platter over her head. She says, "Hey, asshole, this is for all the checks that have bounced," before slamming the platter down in the center of the dining room floor, laughing uproariously as she does so. The sound is brilliant; tiny bits of glass ricochet with dexterity. Inspired, two of the bussers take up dinner plates and send them across the tile like rocks skipped across flat, dull surfaces of water; shards of daisy-imprinted ceramic skitter beneath tables and chairs. A girl I've never seen before cuts herself while walking barefoot. Crossing the dining room on her way to locate another drink, she hops on a single foot, leaving a bloody trail that I imagine animals would sniff at, hunting her. People are leaving the restaurant with actual kitchen equipment. One guy is busy lugging out the KitchenAid mixer before realizing he's too drunk, the mixer's too heavy, the entire situation is a lost cause. He abandons the mixer on table thirteen, taking up the votive and the salt and pepper shakers instead, tucking them in the pocket of his flannel jacket. A very thin girl in skinny jeans has red wine splashed across her white t-shirt as if the bottle vomited on her. She swings a worn muffin tin in her hand. "I think I've always wanted one of these," she slurs to no one in particular. "I'm sure I need one of these, really. Okay?" A tall man whose beard resembles rodents' tails glued to his chin leaves with an entire case of Deschutes porter. Still others huddle in the kitchen near the sliding racks, eating the last of the raspberry crumbles with an animal intensity, their lips and teeth stained a dark blue. They gorge themselves like raccoons, smiling their ferocious blue smiles, and it's then, looking into the East Coast bar, the New York bar, that I notice Jon's favorite painting. Where Flossie's squarish, unrelenting eyes used to be are two giant gashes.

84

Someone has carved a hole in her neck in a clumsy tracheotomy. She has the look, now, of a deranged jack-o'-lantern. Thumb-tacked to Flossie's bell-shaped body are the remains of the employee bulletin board. At the curve of her red hip is a reminder to take the glass recycling out at the beginning of each shift.

Vi appears at 4 a.m., tapping on the front window, her face looking abnormally gaunt and serious. She's shivering, and wearing pajamas. Her eyes have the sagging, dark suggestion of no sleep. Someone lets her in, and soon she is stalking through broken glass and between the overturned tables and chairs, coming for me. I've been smoking a cigarette; I feel momentarily terrified by, first her presence, then her hand, grabbing my wrist.

Lodging her chin on my shoulder, surveying the landscape of destruction, she says, "This is what happens when people hate you. This is what happens when you fail."

The next morning, when I go to pick up my last paycheck, what Jon says to me is, "So, I deducted some money, you know, for damages. Flossie got her eyes poked out last night. Among other things." There is the sound in his voice that I remember from various girlfriends when they learned I'd done something I shouldn't have, right before they called it quits.

"Right," I say. From where I stand, I can't see Vi in the car, but I imagine her, impatiently shifting her weight, tilting down the rearview mirror so that she can examine herself. I imagine her plucking out gray hairs as she waits. Today, she's driving me different places to drop off my résumé so I don't have to worry about parking, about meters and tickets. She worked on my résumé this morning, crafting an articulate objective, checking the capitalization and punctuation, making it as pretty as a black-and-white document about my dismal work history could be. She did this while I slept in, the bedroom curtains pulled tightly closed, a t-shirt wrapped twice around my head to keep out even the most renegade ray of light. I would have slept all day, but she'd tapped on my ribcage, jerked the t-shirt from around my head, and said no, we were doing this.

"Do you have any leads?" Jon asks, casually, and I tell him, casually, yes I do, an interview at a new restaurant in an old hotel in Berkeley. The position is for a breakfast line cook position, eighteen dollars an hour. I don't like to eat eggs, let alone cook them, but Vi spoke slowly to me, as if I had learning difficulties: *eighteen dollars an hour to cook eggs.* She meant, in this economy, this was something to snatch up. She meant, it doesn't matter whether it's interesting to you; it doesn't matter if you actually want to do it. I imagined, at any moment, she might produce eighteen square blocks out of her pocket, adding them up before me, emphasizing her point.

Jon sips from his tiny cup of espresso. He tells me a story, something about an orgy at this hotel in the late '70s, people holed up in the lobby forced to have sex with one another at gunpoint while a madman watched, waving the gun about his head like an irate cowboy. I have no idea if this is true or not, but it's his story, the last one he chooses to tell me.

"You know," he says, "they were forced to give one another blow jobs. Just like that, in front of everyone." He finishes his espresso, holding his pinkie out as he does, and something about his effeminate pinkie pointing at me as he sips makes me want to punch him. In the olden days, I would have. That is, in the days before my fiancée and her white, staring lip scar, in the days before his restaurant with its leaks and inconsistencies and incongruities. Before even the days of Maya and her countless identities, the largeness of her body, and our mistakes together. I would have cracked Jon's jaw against the side of his prized granite countertop; I would have kicked his ribs with the ferocity of police in bad movies kicking down whatever impedes their progress. I would have gone straight through the back door, in the opposite direction of my fiancée sitting in her car, in the opposite direction of those freshly printed résumés placed neatly in the leather folder she bought for the occasion. I would have had a drink; I would have had several. I wouldn't have given two shits about failing or not failing, and it wouldn't have crossed my mind to apologize for any of it.

Outside, tapping on the car's passenger window for Vi to let me in, it occurs to me the tapping could be Morse Code, my own version of SOS. When she finally leans across the seat to unlock the door, her face ruffles at the incessant tapping. *What the hell*, she mouths through the glass. "What the hell?" she asks a second time, because I am still tapping, and it's impossible for me to answer, to say whether this tapping is a true sign of adulthood and of progress, or something so convoluted even she would not have the words for it.

# MONSIEUR

My mother tells me that my old school, with its yellow painted brick, was bulldozed after the new school was built. A cloud of smoke grew up around it, and it was gone. Neighbors held the sweaty hands of their children and watched the crumbling from a safe distance. They ate snacks.

"I'm sorry," my mother says.

"It's all right," I tell her. "Really."

We are in the car, heading home from errands. When we drive by the new school, its windows are black glass like the windows of limousines containing private people who do not want to be seen but who wish to see. I look for students until I remember it's July.

"What do you think?" my mother asks. "Izzy, what do you think?"

When my mother does not receive answers to the questions she's asked, she chews her bottom lip so that her face caves like a soft spot in the earth. Recently, she looks at me with steady eyes, afraid to follow the curve of my elbow to my wrist, to those certain raw scars, just as she asks questions in nervous strings so that I think of paper dolls when they are finally pulled open: not one body but a series of bodies with connecting hands, or rather, wrists. With each fold there is another doll, another doll. With my mother, there is always another question.

*Izzy, what have you done?* she has asked during these days, these weeks, I've been home, her voice puncturing our polite routine: the bank, the dry cleaner's, morning game shows, afternoon talk shows, tuna melts made with opaque sliced tomatoes denying the vibrancy of summer. *Why did you do this? What were you thinking? Izzy, do you ever think?*

I have answered that I haven't done anything. I have answered, yes, I think. I am careful not to let these things sound like questions.

The first day of class in the building with the yellow painted brick was late in August, the morning filled with lingering heat. He stood in front of the classroom dressed in a long black trench coat, a bright red turtleneck spilling over its neckline. His left hand clutched the brim of his hat as if he'd just stumbled inside a traumatic wind. He was Mr. Rock, though everyone called him *Monsieur Roche,* the literal translation of his name into French. I'd heard the stories: how he believed himself a cat in a former life; how he jumped when students sprayed water at him with guns snuck into class as a prank. Rumor said he never bathed, that he wore the same pants every day, pin-striped and grease spotted. The turtleneck, rumor said, was actually a dickey, and this word I looked up in the library's dictionary to discover a dickey was a false shirt front, a detachable bosom. Reference was made to something called "the flapping dickey."

On that morning, Monsieur's red dickey remained unflappable. From a corner of the classroom came strangled sounds like those of a cat trapped beneath the hood of a car. Monsieur stood before us as if deciding, just as he might with a malodorous and weepy piece of garbage, what exactly to do with us. When the clock ticked finally to 10 a.m., Monsieur did not sit in the teacher's chair, a comfortable seat with thick padded armrests bespeaking authority. He pulled a tiny student's desk to the front of the room and forced himself into it. The act was reminiscent of a child trying to fit a too-large square inside a too-small circle. His arms clacked like chicken wings. His skin, gray, appeared shaded, like an unfortunate freshman art assignment. I did not yet know that I would spend weeks in Studio Art I replicating a dismal still life (dented guitar, lopsided apple, shorn shawl) while the instructor spoke ambiguously about "creative problem solving." Happiness appeared incomprehensible. It appeared incomprehensible that this man could speak a beautiful language.

*Je m'appelle Monsieur Roche.*

His voice, deep and textured with secrets, unraveled like a luxurious carpet I might spill something on and afterward be reprimanded for. His voice thumbed each word as if it were velveteen; was a voice so compelling I overlooked his bad habit: he tugged at the dirty lobe of his ear as he spoke.

Another habit, though it took days, nearly weeks, for me to both recognize and admit it: his eyes traveled the length and width of the classroom with its bare bulletin boards—for Monsieur had not hung a single dull rendering of the Arc de Triomphe, the river Seine, the tour Eiffel; had not produced a single crumpled crepe-paper border or a proclamation on either student hygiene or the degenerating effects of drugs on our pink pliable brains—and settled on me, the skin above his eyes kneaded as unattractively as the lumps of dough we pummeled on a floured surface in home economics.

Who was I? Tiny inside my own desk, I curled myself like a leaf above its surface, close enough to smell its lacquer. *Belma, Belle, Isabelle, Izzy*, these the rattling transmutations of my name in others' voices. I had pale skin even though summer had barely ended. It is a bald fact: I have never liked the sun.

My mother says that I should spend more time outside. She claims I need the sun, its irrefutable benefits, its Vitamin D.

"Its cancerous inclinations," I add.

She spreads a towel across the driveway, where she lies on her stomach, toes curled into the sweltering asphalt. She forgets to lotion the bottoms of her feet. They burn, although the rest of her tans nicely. From the shade of the porch, I watch her become the color of a churro.

"Izzy, if you took the sweatshirt off." My mother speaks recently in parts of sentences, sentence fragments disguised as whole sentences. Hers are broken sentences, as if someone has made off with their heads, their elbows, their rutted clavicles. I have imagined their fragile remains buried deep within the earth, between beloved pets and time capsules.

"I'm completely cool," I say. "Nearly frigid."

My mother is a woman who believes in multitasking. While she tans, she also brews sun tea.

"You shouldn't do that," I say. "Bacteria proliferates."

"Old wives' tale!" my mother says. "Ridiculous! Next you'll tell me I shouldn't turn a loaf of bread upside down once it has a slice taken from it."

"I have no idea about the bread," I say. "But the ropy strands will kill you." And because the word *kill* is now a sensitive one between us, taboo, the tea with its ropy strands disappears down the kitchen sink with a flush of water.

At the shore where we occasionally visited during summers, I stayed in the dark corners of the motel room reading the sheer pages of the Bible I'd found in the dresser, Leviticus and Deuteronomy, stories of sin and worship, while my mother paced the boardwalk alone, ate cotton candy, paid fifty cents to lift a rubber duck from its never-ending rectangle of manmade river. She boasted of her ability to win the water-shooting games, claimed to put myriad fathers to shame. It pained her that I never witnessed her prowess.

My own father was not a man who played water games. When I saw him during these summers, he spoke from inside his starched white dress shirts and beige suits, a man who did not understand the concept of irony. "Look at you, Belle, so pale. Get yourself some color."

Monsieur carried a red duffel bag to class. Each morning he drew a perfume bottle from inside this duffel bag and saturated the air with a strong, sweet smell that burned our lungs. This scent traveled by slow osmosis to us, students coughing and dramatically covering their mouths. The bottle itself was beautiful, cut with different shapes of deeply colored glass—sparkling burgundy, sparkling emerald—and every morning Monsieur reminded us he'd found this bottle in France, inside a tiny shop on a rutted country road, a place where they hadn't known its real value and where he'd gotten it for a steal.

"Yes, a steal," he said, tugging at his ear.

From inside this red duffel he also pulled a thermos each morning, pausing midsentence to hold up the thermos lid, which served as a cup, and say, "I don't believe I've thanked you for my tea this morning. Thank you, thank you for this tea. Dragonwell, Longjing. It's lovely. You are terribly kind for allowing me to imbibe it."

One September morning before class, several students hovered over a single desk in their Shetland sweaters, blinking eyelids swabbed in profuse pink shadow and whispering: should they slip a tab of acid inside Monsieur's tea? Would he be thankful for it then?

"What do you think, Belma?" My name in their voices sounded like either a painful cough or a cry for help. From inside the round comfort of their laughter, they stared at me: a girl in a hideous floral top intently coloring the negative space of the letters in her French homework as a means of avoiding their eyes.

"Do you know how to speak?" a girl asked from beneath a heap of teased bangs. "Can you even fucking speak?"

"Thank you, Mother," I say, these words the refrain when she has cleared my dinner plate, setting it in the sink with a clatter that tells me she is annoyed I haven't cleared it myself.

"Thank you, Mother," I say when a lull in the conversation looms up, loudly, or when the volume on the television dips unexpectedly lower and I feel the acute need to fill the air with something.

"Thank you, Mother." We sit together on the couch, she painting her nails with even strokes.

"Stop it, Izzy."

"What?"

"Berating me," she says. "Stop berating me."

"I have no idea what you're talking about."

"Why don't you wear nail polish?" she asks. "Why don't you wear makeup? A woman your age, Izzy, should wash her face. A woman your age should brush her hair. She should be wary of things like unibrows. The men in your department would appreciate a woman who gave some thought to her appearance."

"The men in my department," I say, "prefer good sentences to eyebrows. They wouldn't know a unibrow if they tripped on it."

My mother snorts into her jar of polish. When she is finished with the painting, she sits like a statue with her fingers spread uncomfortably apart like a jazz dancer in a variety show. She asks will I pour her a glass of diet soda, not too much ice. She asks will I change the television channel.

I flip to Russian news on one of the cable channels. Words fall from the newscaster's mouth like incongruous pebbles.

"Now, Izzy," my mother says. "Even that woman wears makeup. That woman, in her distant and impoverished country, looks more put together than you, Isabelle."

"Yes, Mother," I say. "I suppose she does."

Those first weeks, we moved briskly through our work. We rolled our *r*'s, sounding like a nest of choking birds. We conjugated *er* verbs and studied basic vocabulary, certain ones of us struggling with the concept of gendered nouns. *Répétez, répétez!* Monsieur demonstrated his perfect pronunciation, and we, sounding like drugged cult members, repeated: *un livre, un vélo, une auto, une caméra, une guitare.* We plowed through *la construction infinitive* and *l'impératif.* We studied *être* and *avoir.* These were irregular verbs, Monsieur said, possibly difficult for us to remember—this seemed like the slightest dig at either the capacity of our brains or the quality of our work ethics—but we would not, Monsieur said, get far without them. *Être,* Monsieur said, a model of pronunciation. To be. *Je suis, tu es, il/elle est, nous sommes, vous êtes, ils/elles sont.* He finished, panting. *Avoir.* To have. The conjugation spit from his mouth without warning. We studied the *ir* verbs with their complicated, sibilant sounds in the second- and third-person plurals. *Finissons, finissez, finissent.*

It was during our Chapter 4 vocabulary quiz that Monsieur interrupted us to ask, Did we know he had walked to New York City?

Several polite students shook their heads while others snickered.

Yes, he had. People had told him he could never do it. New York was precisely 120.7 miles from Scranton: a two-hour drive by car, three-and-a-half by Greyhound. Still, he left his apartment on Adam's Avenue with his red duffel bag to hold his food, following the highway to New York, that glistening and debauched apple.

"Here, a person can do such a thing as sleep on the grass. Our lovely state is conducive to such behavior. Others, not so much. Perhaps you have all heard of chiggers? *Parasites irritables!*" Monsieur patiently counted his fingers and said, "It took four days to make the trip."

"But did you walk back?" someone asked, and a voice answered with a mocking meow.

Monsieur wrangled himself from his tiny student's desk. He stood at the window, staring at the orange and red and yellow leaves shaking on the trees. I watched the second hand complete three full revolutions before he turned around and asked, in the manner of a surprised fairy godmother brandishing a wand, "Yes! What were we thinking of?"

Our vocabulary quiz resumed with vigor. Chapter 4 centered on the verb *avoir*, sturdy little expressions for everyday living. To be hot: *avoir chaud*. To be hungry: *avoir faim*. Prior to his story, Monsieur had just ticked off numbers eight and nine. To be sleepy, *avoir sommeil*. To be right, *avoir raison*. Now he said, "Number ten, *fabaceous*." We stared blankly at our papers. "Number eleven, *nachtmaal*. Number twelve, *sarangousty*."

Several hands shot up around the room. Monsieur interrupted himself again: Did we know *why* he had told us that story?

Someone said, "Because you're crazy?"

Monsieur snapped his head toward this voice and said, "To prove that I am capable of anything! Anything!"

The room split open with our silence. Monsieur took careful sips of tea and did not thank us.

Toward the end of October, Monsieur started opening the windows before class. "It's autumn!" he said. "*C'est l'automne*. The most beautiful time of the year!"

"Everything's dying," someone said. "What isn't dead, is dying."
*"Imbécile!"* Monsieur muttered beneath his breath. *"Stupide!"*

We endured the cold, the least resilient of us raising our hands for hall passes to retrieve our coats. Gusts of wind whisked falling leaves into the classroom, and these leaves settled in the aisles, on desktops. Leaves crunched beneath shoes whenever students walked to the pencil sharpener or left class to use the restroom. Red and orange and yellow wisps tossed themselves inside the air as we conjugated verbs.

"We'll watch a little bit of a French movie every day," Monsieur said one morning, plucking a yellow leaf from the fat collar of his turtleneck. He gestured grandiosely to the VCR a boy was wheeling into the room. "This way you'll hear the sounds of the language."

On this occasion, Monsieur spent the duration of class pushing buttons and jiggling the wires running from the VCR to the television. Having heard not a syllable of French, we shuffled from the classroom slowly, leaving Monsieur to whirl his fingers mysteriously before the blank screen as if this strange motion might nudge it to life.

The next class, Monsieur asked someone to help him. It pained him to do so. "Yes," he said. "There are complications. This very foul machine refuses to work properly. Possibly, I should demand another."

A boy changed the television to the correct channel with a quick flick of his wrist.

We watched *Un homme et une femme.* Monsieur canted the television stand toward himself, and the students on the right side of the room could not see the screen. They asked, Could Monsieur turn the television toward them, *s'il vous plaît?* He ignored them, sitting so precariously in his tiny student's desk I expected him at any moment to tip forward, break like an egg against the floor. In the dark—blinds drawn but rattling before the open windows—I studied his crackable fragility.

Sensing my stare, he jerked his head toward me; I jerked my own away.

For several days, we watched this movie the last ten minutes of class, beginning at the part before the first love scene blinked across the screen, a subtle howl of wind in the background, the steady beating of a heart in the foreground, Monsieur keeping his head in time with the beats.

We watched this love scene once, twice, three times. On the fourth day, a student asked, "Haven't we seen this part before?"

Monsieur forced a clipped smile. "*Mais non.*"

A voice in the back of the room said, "We're tired of watching porn!"

Another asked, "We are?"

Monsieur pushed buttons on the VCR until, finally, the image disappeared and static crackled noisily. He did not turn the volume lower, or click the television off. We sat listening to the static, watching its gray and white dance across the screen, for nearly ten minutes until the bell rang. I closed my eyes and imagined we were inside an airplane, something broken, going down.

At lunch, I avoided the cafeteria. I walked instead through the sleek hallways smelling of disinfectant to the library, passing the faculty room whose door remained chronically slung open. Monsieur did not sit with the other teachers, gossiping about which student had failed what or who had uttered what inane comment. He never hovered over a mint-green cafeteria tray filled with that day's enticing choices: various penile-shaped meats cooked on a stick, fruit cocktail comprised of slithery pineapple and engorged cherries, limp fries. He never possessed the flattened sandwiches that other teachers pulled from crumpled lunch bags. He ate nothing, sitting alone in a corner of the room with a book balanced across his knees in an act of grace and dexterity that transfixed me. Monsieur was an intent reader but once, twice, our eyes caught as I passed.

And then, one day, he waited outside the faculty room door.

"*Bonjour*, Belma," he said, and something inside me shook; I'd never heard him address a student outside of class.

"*Bonjour.*" I mustered as much beauty as I could with that single word. Mine were long legs, and I forged ahead, wondering what to possibly say to him if he remained beside me.

"Belma," he said, and together we stopped walking. "Do you like to read?"

The hallway contained its typical echoing darkness, but the fire door's neat rectangular window at the end opened into an acute brightness that I imagined was akin to the brightness of death nearing.

"Of course you like to read," he answered himself. "I sense that about you. There are certain things a person can tell."

Monsieur continued. He loved to read, though he refrained from saying what writing he liked. He'd begun reading when he was two years old (yes, two!) and had read so many things since then. He could not categorize such a thing as writing.

"It's human nature, I suppose, to categorize. It's their grandest coping mechanism, aside from being cruel. It's how they manage." He, too, stood staring at the bright, beckoning light at the end of the hallway. "Yes, a book a week since I was two. If I didn't . . ." An elongated pause passed while he studied me with glassine eyes. "Then a week would not be the same."

I nodded.

"I once headed both the French and English departments. That was a long time ago, Belma. Before countless things."

Silence swelled around us, punctuated by distant slamming lockers. A student wearing clacking penny loafers emerged from the depths of the hallway carrying a fluttering hall pass.

"I'm published in *The New Yorker*," Monsieur said once the student had disappeared. "Under an anonymous name, of course, because I'd rather people didn't know. You've probably read my writing countless times and you've never once known it was me."

"I've never read *The New Yorker*," I said.

"I trust, Belma," Monsieur said, "that you are above *Anne of Green Gables*."

"Yes!" I said, though in fact I had cried uncontrollably when, in the last book of the series, Anne's son Walter died on the battlegrounds of World War I, these tears causing my mother to say, "It's just a book, Izzy."

"What I wanted to tell you: your papers are beautifully written. Your mastery of the language at this early stage . . . *magnifique*. Your pronunciation . . ." He did not have an adjective for my pronunciation. This description he abandoned to the sounds of the hallway.

"You don't talk in my classroom. The others, they have no respect. I have never seen you laugh at me. You're an excellent student. And do you know what?"

I shook my head.

"We've escaped! We're done for the week!" Monsieur smiled, his mouth growing unusually large, as if he'd previously been suppressing the size of it. This smile, huge, dipped off his face as he said, "Thank you, Belma, sincerely. Thank you. Until next week, then."

I watched as he walked toward the fire door and its bright rectangle. I knew that he would trudge across the pavement to the unwieldy brush on the opposite side of the road, where the school's nonsmoking rule did not apply. I'd seen him while I waited for the afternoon bus, standing in the overgrowth, drawing the cigarette to his mouth with surprising fluidity. His gray face stared anomalously from the jagged leaves like something in a surrealist painting, his red turtleneck dickey providing the only true jolt of color.

"Look at him hiding in there." A student had pointed out Monsieur's face in the brush with an acute shiver. "Like some disgusting animal."

My mother and I are in the kitchen when she fills up a glass of water that bubbles over because I've used too much dish detergent, have not rinsed the glass out properly.

"Do you see?" She laughs and touches my shoulder, dumps the water into the sink. "You'll kill me."

"Yes," I tell her, and am joking. "But not until I kill myself."

She falls quiet. And then she is clattering glasses and forks, filling up the silence between us.

These are the lyrics between the refrains.

✳   ✳   ✳

The last thing we learned in French, although it was not the end of the school year, was the difference in usage between the *passé composé* and the *imparfait*.

"We use these tenses," Monsieur said, "to talk about the past."

In French, he said, the *passé composé* was used for actions completed at a specific time in the past. These actions were done, finished. The *imparfait* was used to describe things that happened repeatedly in the past, habitual actions. Or it was used for descriptive passages that served only to set a scene.

Our last homework assignment involved the *passé composé* and the *imparfait*. We ripped our papers from our workbooks, passed them to the front of the room. Monsieur slid these papers inside the red duffel bag and said, "Yes, I will return them tomorrow."

These events might typically have been written in the *imparfait*: they had occurred every day, in precisely this same manner, since the first day of class. Except that on this particular day, the papers Monsieur slid inside his duffel bag were never to be seen again. The next morning, rather than return our assignments as he had always done, Monsieur announced that from now on we would watch movies. "I have laryngitis, you know," he said, his voice sounding as smooth and rich as it always had. "It is impossible for me to educate you in this manner. Until this problem resolves, we will devote our studies to film."

We watched old American films Monsieur prefaced with rambling synopses. He introduced *The Razor's Edge* by acknowledging that Gene Tierney was "a beautiful woman, flawed only by the presence of an overbite that makes her—in my humble opinion—only more perfect in light of this hovering imperfection. This woman had a difficult time, suffering from mental illness as she did and receiving nearly twenty-seven shock treatments in her lifetime. She was married to the illustrious Oleg Cassini. Their first daughter was born severely retarded, no thanks to a sick fan who left quarantine to procure Ms. Tierney's autograph. Alas, she was pregnant at the time. It doomed their marriage. Oleg Cassini designed the lovely

Jacqueline Bouvier Kennedy's clothing. Perhaps you recollect her attire on the day of her husband's inauguration. The other women wore fur and resembled wild buffalo waiting to be slaughtered, but thanks to Oleg, Jacqueline looked so sleek and modern. There was a woman with lovely knees!" Regarding *On the Waterfront*: "And it was Brando, beautiful Brando, who made the white t-shirt so ubiquitous. Prior to his appearance in *A Streetcar Named Desire*—yes, we'll get to that one, hopefully before Christmas break, as it is, indeed, a gift— white t-shirts were worn only by professional wrestlers. Speaking of Brando, he is a magnificent actor, but if you watch him in later movies, you will understand why we place importance on such a thing as a healthful diet. Please, consult the food pyramid."

These screenings ended one day when, arriving to class, we found Monsieur seated at his tiny student's desk. Taped to its edge was a sign written in his quivering calligraphic hand: *Do Not Disturb*. The clock ticked past the start of class, and Monsieur remained seated, eyes closed, an index finger shoved inside each ear, hands jutting from either side of his temple like unfurled wings.

*Do Not Disturb.*


My mother believes in excursions. This is a recent development— that we frequent places that demand ticket stubs and plastic wrist-tags for entry. She collects these things as proof of our relationship, of time spent together.

At the State Park, we rent paddleboats that we don't actually paddle. We float, the sun blaring like something unmistakably loud.

"Isn't this nice?" my mother asks. "Isn't this beautiful?" From our spot on the water, I hear the unrelenting cries of children in the public swimming pool. Flies nudge. Sweat pools.

On another afternoon as sweltering as a sauna, my mother drives us along Route 6 to the Archbald Pothole, where we lean over the railing, peering down its thirty-eight feet.

People like to throw things inside the Archbald Pothole, she tells me. Officials have pulled out traffic cones, a ten-speed bicycle, the bent hood of a car. Once, this place was a hotbed of illicit activity.

On one occasion, my mother tells me, twenty-nine men were arrested for lewd behavior during a single police sweep.

"They're trying hard," she says, "to make this a place for families."

"The family that visits potholes together, stays together." I laugh into the sultry air.

"We're a family," my mother says, "and *we're* here."

She has brought bagged lunches that we eat at a splintered picnic table. We swipe the insides of our sweaty knees in between bites of our limp lunch-meat sandwiches, and I refrain from telling her this is not hygienic.

We descend three hundred feet below the earth on the Lackawanna Coal Mine Tour, my mother shivering and pulling her sweater tightly around herself as we listen to a man in a hardhat speak beneath the glare of a naked lightbulb. The organizers of this tour have decided we want Entertainment Value. Entertainment Value equates to mannequins reenacting historical scenes. A mannequin with a coal-dusted face leads a donkey into the depths of the mine. A hand shakes from inside a mound of gravel, demonstrating the catastrophes in mining and the horrors of being buried alive.

"Look at that!" my mother says. Behind her, water drips and anthracite glistens. Sharpened pieces abound, shards you could gouge your own heart with.

I ask, "This is the best northeastern Pennsylvania has to offer?"

"I'm trying, Izzy," my mother says. Leaning forward, she grasps the shaking hand as though for comfort. It shudders inside her clasp, unable to stand her touch. "Can't you see I'm trying?"

"Please," a man in a hard hat upbraids my mother. "You can't touch the displays."


The day that he first called me Chantal was the Wednesday before Thanksgiving break. I was last leaving the classroom, and he called the name quietly but quickly, like a muted cough. Because I was the only one in the room, I turned to him.

"I would like to call you that," Monsieur said. "It's my favorite French name. It suits you. It's beautiful."

I had thought the name was beautiful the first time I saw it, printed in the introductory dialogues at the beginning of each chapter in our French book. Scribbled pictures of Chantal accompanied these dialogues. Chantal had an electric mass of hair and wide eyes that made her look deranged. She was remarkably industrious: in a single drawing in the first chapter, she telephoned her friends, did her homework, listened to the radio, and ate dinner. In another, she danced in leg warmers that engulfed her tiny legs (Chantal *danse*.) She swam, her cartoon arms lunging like imperfect C's from the water. (Chantal *nage*.) Chantal had scribbled boyfriends named Jean-Luc and Claude who wore their shirts unbuttoned to their navels and with whom she frequently attended *la discothèque*. Together, they consumed voracious amounts of *les frites* and *Le Coke*.

"Belma," Monsieur said. "Where did your mother find such a name?"

"My father chose it," I said. "It was his grandmother's name."

"I'm sure," Monsieur said, apologetically, "I'm certain she was a lovely woman. I mean no disregard to her."

"I never met her," I said. "I have no idea. She might have been awful."

"Henceforth," Monsieur said. "Henceforth, you will be Chantal."

"Yes," I said. "Okay."

Silence bloomed between us. The clock ticked, tocked, ticked. Monsieur shifted his weight, tugged at his ear. He wrangled with something, deliberated it. Finally, taking a big breath, he plunged forward, not unlike someone plunging forth into the swells of the ocean, determined to enjoy it.

"Our relationship, Chantal, is so very important. It's what I have subsisted on these twenty difficult years, when it seemed impossible to subsist on anything at all. When it seemed, possibly, I might curl up and die!"

"I know that," I chose to say; understood to say. "I do."

"For twenty years," Monsieur said, "you have been my salvation! Thank you. *Thank you.*" Bringing my hand clumsily to his chapped lips, he kissed it.

\* \* \*

We spent lunch inside the classroom, each of us sitting inside a tiny student's desk facing the window and the cold, rattling branches of the trees bracing themselves for winter. Outside, snow fell. The heaters wheezed out their dry, desperate heat.

"You remember, Chantal, the actress who wanted your part in *Tartuffe*. She tried sabotaging you in so many ways, but of course she could never touch you. And that wonderful night of your standing ovation! I saw her reaction. If she'd had a martini glass in her hand like she was so fond of having, she would have smashed it into a million easy bits on the floor! She never amounted to anything, you know. Years later, she remained a bit actress in bit roles. She lived like a pauper! Her skin appeared utterly ravaged."

"She was beautiful, too, in her day," I said.

"She was nothing!" Monsieur bristled, slammed his hand against the desk. "Oh, God, nothing!"

I learned that Chantal looked ravishing (*ravissant!*) in the long pink gown and pristine white elbow gloves she donned for dinner on the rue de Rivoli. Never ceasing to entertain, she sometimes wore theater costumes to dinner. Dressed as a Renaissance trollop, she passed between the tables in a tiny restaurant on the rue de la Paix, bumping people's knees with her wide skirt, her lovely breasts held hostage by the gown's bodice. She frequently tossed her expensive shoes to the street at the end of a long night, walking the cobblestones barefoot, his jacket coddling her shoulders. The fine nape of her neck presented the perfect place to lay a beautiful piece of sapphire jewelry, had he possessed the means to purchase such a thing. His hand was her finest accessory, clasping her neck and guiding her through the Paris streets at night. She had perfect arches and could have been a ballerina, had she chosen. She loved to dance!

Once, like Cinderella, she'd lost a shoe at a party; not a glass slipper, but velveteen.

"She was always kicking them off, anyway," I said, lapsing forgetfully into Belma, and Monsieur ignored this impertinence.

"Yes, Chantal, everything disappeared at midnight. But you regret leaving New York, don't you?"

"Yes!"

"I thought you did." Monsieur nodded. "Though I understand, those were such difficult times. That tiny apartment, the cold. Those insidious bugs!" He shuddered, thinking of them.

"I know now I shouldn't have given it up for all the world," I said. "I'm sorry."

"Yes, I have always known you were." A pause. "Tell me, Chantal, was he that special? Oh, he was handsome! I was many things at the time, but not blind! I could appreciate his good looks, those shoulders, the fact that he could provide. But tell me, did you truly love him?"

"No," I said. "I did not."

"I thought not," he said. "I was certain of it." His hand fluttered to my knobby knee.

One day Monsieur said, "You don't eat."

"You know I have to be extremely thin for the theater," I said. "You know how competitive it is! You've told me to never let down my guard!"

His voice sliced through the air. "I have never seen you, Belma, eat."

He brought things for us to share. I had once imagined Monsieur ate only canned dinners, things found inside a disaster survival kit, processed and immediate, things you'd eat only if you found yourself on the point, the sheer precipice, of death and chaos. I'd imagined, given his dealings with the VCR, specifically regarding the issue of tracking, that Monsieur could scarcely boil water without crying into it, distraught it had not heated as quickly as he wished. Regarding food, Monsieur was not incapable. He ate meticulously, a starched white napkin spread across his lap, a second stashed beside him for the constant wiping of his mouth. We ate baguettes with *jambon* and *fromage,* and Monsieur detailed, carefully, each of the cheeses we ate.

"This, Belma, is Brillat-Savarin. Triple cream, cow's milk. Named after a truly brilliant man. Perhaps you've read *The Physiology of Taste?*" (I had not.) "It's shameful we don't have champagne to pair with it, but in this godforsaken place, we'll make do as best we can.

This, Belma, is Explorateur. Seventy-five percent fat! A gem!" On the topic of Neufchâtel, which came heart-shaped, he said, without a tinge of irony, "How darling! How sweet!" He poked at the rind as I'd seen women poke at the fat knees of babies.

Days passed before Monsieur succumbed to temptation—bringing wine in the thermos he normally reserved for tea.

"Trust I know the integrity of this wine is compromised! But it's the only way in this culture, with its haphazard rules. The authorities would haul me off if they knew! Drinking wine with a student! You must never tell a soul about any of it. These are our secrets. Drink, Belma, drink," he said.

I lifted the lid to my mouth, the wine dipped forward. I didn't like it, not at all, but I lacked the heart to tell Monsieur, who waxed poetic until the bell rang: tobacco and spice box, mellow tannins and French oak, Saint-Julien-Beychevelle, where he passed two luminous weeks in the summer of 1974.

"My mother drinks pink wine from a box," I said, and Monsieur stared at me, horrified, over the lip of the thermos lid.

"Frequently," I added, and Monsieur said, "Oh, Belma!"

"Your mother," he said. "I imagined her to be such a dignified woman. I imagined, thinking of her, that the apple did not fall very far from the tree. It must take an astounding woman, I thought, to produce this curious, wonderful child."

On this occasion, we shared an apple smeared with a particularly luscious Camembert. Monsieur typically snorted at clichés, but this one fell fluidly from his mouth as he sawed a slice of apple.

"In this case," I said, "the apple resides somewhere else entirely. Possibly, the apple resides in France. Or Lebanon," I said. "The apple resides in Lebanon."

"I see," Monsieur said.

He could not believe I ate the entire apple, seeds and all. He laughed when he said, "There's cyanide in each seed, Belma. Only very small amounts, but still."

"How many apple seeds would it take?" I asked.

Monsieur said, "You are not a happy child."

I shook my head vigorously.

"Yes, you can tell me, Belma."

"No." Beyond the window, a bird pecked at the hard ground. "There is nothing to say."

It was cold, cold December when Monsieur showed me his scars, rolling up the sleeves of his trench coat until they resembled fat doughnuts circling his elbows. These scars webbed his arms like highways seen from the window of an ascending airplane, reminiscent of the meandering red route lines on the road maps we practiced reading in third grade. A person, closing their eyes and touching them, could read their stories as easily as Braille.

"I thought it was best," I said, "to cut horizontally." At age fourteen, this was my idea of a joke. There was no cheese on this particular occasion, not even something hard and aged, enlivened by membrillo. There was only a quickly fading daylight, a winter storm warning. Snow fell, fell, fell. Monsieur's face resembled a boulder the moment before it rolled off a craggy edge.

"Belma," he said, grasping my wrist tightly, "you listen to me."

Outside, the snow performed its slow dance of accumulation.

"Those were dark times. Dark, very dark times. Similar to residing in a closet devoid of light, subsisting on mung beans and stale water. You are familiar with the story of Patricia Hearst and the Symbionese Liberation Army."

I was not.

"Like being buried alive," he said. "That ceaseless weight of disaster and disappointment. That, truly, is how it felt."

When I pulled my wrist away, a red mark remained, a warning sign that quickly faded.

"Trying times," he said. "Impossible!"

Taking up my hands, he spoke his next words into them with heated breath. "I survived, Belma, and so will you."

The last day Monsieur walked into the classroom (*passé composé*, an emphatic tense), a plastic tub of water waited on his desk. Stacked beside this tub, erected like a child's toy, stood several towers of soap bars.

He asked, "What is this?"

A single voice choked out the beginning of a laugh.

"It's your bath," a high mock-voice said. "We brought you a bath."

Like a bean, Monsieur's voice jumped. "Who's going to get rid of it?"

Students stared forward, palms folded neatly on their desks. From inside this careful scene, someone said, "Freak!"

"*Le* freak!" someone corrected.

Silence elongated, quivered. Monsieur stared for a long time at the plastic tub. Then, with sudden frenzied movement, he opened a classroom window. Handling each bar of soap as if it was something dangerous, Monsieur threw them one by one into the soft white snow. Plunk, plunk, plunk. It was no surprise that Monsieur threw like a girl, with an unnatural, uncomfortable flexion in his wrist and an exaggerated stance. Below his too-short pants, his ankles shook.

"Belma," he said when he had finished. "Take this down to the maintenance room."

A hiss from the desk behind me. "Don't do it!"

A second hiss. "She will!"

Monsieur looked away from the tub with the same angle to his chin that my mother had when she saw live surgeries performed on television, mounds of organs pulsating beneath shiny instruments and the masked faces of doctors. Water slopped over the sides when I picked it up. I had not imagined how heavy water could be. I had not imagined how weak I was. My arms trembled. Water thrashed. I saw now what I had not seen from my desk: a single rubber ducky bobbed gracefully on the water's surface, its frozen blue eyes evaluating the situation at hand.

"Open the door for her," Monsieur directed. "Help her."

On the tops of desks hands remained folded, immobile.

"We hate her," someone snickered. "We hate you."

Monsieur touched the doorknob as if it might burn his skin. He refused to look at me as I stumbled over the threshold. The water inside the tub shifted its weight, righted itself. The classroom door closed loudly, and I was alone, an endless polished floor before me, beckoning, shiny and expectant. The maintenance room was a long hallway, a left, and two rights away. I inched toward the bright smacking sunlight glinting through the fire doors at the end of the hall. The plastic tub tumbled and crashed; water slid across the linoleum away from me.

I did not return to class. I walked home in ankle-deep snow, bootless, coatless, hatless, plunging one foot in front of the other, walking the cold miles away from there.

The denouement happened that night. *Dénouement*: that is a French word, stemming from *desnouer*, to untie; stemming from Latin, *nodus*, knot.

My mother, coming home from work, discovered me facedown on the couch, sobbing.

"What is it, Izzy?" Her voice carried its impatience carefully, like something she might balance on her head.

I had not yet become a girl who sobbed. This was perhaps the beginning of my intimate relationship with sobbing, its relentless pricking of a person's pale insides. I was not yet familiar with its jagged arresting of breath, the headache starting in the back of the skull and moving insistently forward.

I sobbed so hard I shook.

I had never told my mother anything; had not yet learned the importance of selective detail, of omission. Once started, I could not stop. I told her about the piercing laughter of the other kids at school; that I was not Belma or Belle or Isabelle or Izzy, but Chantal, who drank Saint Julien from the lid of a thermos, who ate the funkiest of nonpasteurized cheeses *avec plaisir*.

A hated girl, a hated girl.

Or perhaps the denouement happened the next day, when Monsieur did not come to class, but the principal did.

The principal was a woman who kept pens at the ready on her person: stuck inside her mouth, tucked behind each ear, shoved inside her bun, holding it up. She sheathed herself in nude: nude pantyhose, nude skirt and blouse, nude pumps, this wash of nude blemished occasionally by ink stains. She resembled the undressed mannequins I'd seen strewn on the floor at the department store, their heads turned demonically, their arms akimbo. The principal was my first lesson, at age fourteen, that women who wear blouses, slacks, and pumps are different from women who wear shirts, pants, and shoes. Some women wear hose; others, stockings. A certain kind of woman believes nude is a color.

The principal said, "Well, today you will not be watching movies." She said, "*Monsieur Roche ne retournerai pas.*"

I raised my hand.

"Yes, Belma."

"That's future tense," I said. "We haven't learned that."

"Where did you leave off, then?" Her voice was a thread, pulling tightly, clustering her words uncomfortably together.

"Page eighty-six," I said.

"Yes." She thumbed to the page. "The *imparfait* and the *passé composé.*"

That night, when I knocked on my mother's bedroom door, she sat at her vanity removing her eye makeup. One eye had been wiped clean, but the other remained thick with black liner and purple shadow. She stared at me with these two faces. "Yes, Isabelle?"

I said, "Monsieur did not come to class."

She cleaned off the other eye and stared at me colorlessly. "So?"

"He's not coming back," I said.

"Does it matter?" she asked.

"Yes."

"No," she said. "It doesn't matter." She examined her vials of lipstick. "I had nothing to do with it."

"I know," I said, and knew she had.

"It's time," my mother said. "You need to fit in. You need to make friends. You don't try, Izzy. Do you understand?"

"Yes, Mother," I said. "I understand."

"Good," she said.

*   *   *

Our last trek of the summer is to a family amusement park.

"Fun!" my mother says, passing through the turnstile. "What fun!"

We shove past sticky children, swat at flies. We are amusement-park voyeurs, pressing our hips against the metal railings, watching others. Children float by on brightly colored ladybugs, their faces awash with uncertainty: does this occasion demand laughter or tears? They steer boats on a calm, circular sea, their fat hands rising to salute their parents as they drift past. Couples are whisked to the sky beneath glistening umbrella tops, the air punctured with their cries. On a tiny stage, Celtic dancers fudge their jigs.

In a shaded pavilion hung with a banner declaring Carfagno Family Reunion!, my mother and I eat pierogi swabbed with butter while members of the Carfagno family dish their twenty-four-hour salad, their macaroni and potato salads, their mysterious casseroles, onto buckling styrofoam plates.

"This is someone's family reunion," I say in a sharpened whisper.

"We're family, too," my mother says. "And it's shaded here."

"Not *this* family," I say.

The Carfagno women sit on folding chairs, lifting first one dimpled thigh and then another. They fan themselves with styrofoam plates. There is a proliferation of beer cozies and terry-cloth shorts. Someone has brought a bucket of KFC. In this palpable, awful heat, the Carfagno women have decided that questioning our presence demands too much energy. They balance their mayonnaised lunches across their naked knees, and the image returns to me with an acute pain: graceful Monsieur in the faculty room, a book balanced on his knees.

The heat, the proximity of the Carfagnos, embolden me. I haven't mentioned Monsieur since that night years ago, but now I say, "He was very kind to me. A friend. The only one I had."

My mother's face registers the conversation topic. She looks as if she's swallowed something very tart. "That was fifteen years ago, Izzy."

"Are you sorry?"

"I'm not sorry, Izzy, for doing what was best for you."

"Belma," I say. "I hate being called Izzy."

My mother snorts. "Or should I call you Chantal, for old times' sake?" She says, "I should probably tell you. He died, Izzy. I saw the obituary in the paper. I would have told you, but you were in college and doing well. You were happy. The paper said nothing about the grandiose life he claimed to have lived. Born and died in Scranton, Pennsylvania. Went to Scranton High, the University of Scranton. No different than me, Izzy. He did nothing. He was a liar if he told you otherwise. And something else," she continues. "The obituary used that vague language that signifies suicide. *Died unexpectedly at home.* Everyone knows what that means. I'm not stupid! You were young, and he implanted ideas in your head!"

"No one implanted anything," I say.

"You're calling me stupid," she says.

"You're not stupid," I say. "But you should know I've never been happy."

I've never seen my mother cry, but she cries now, a sloppy kind of crying, replete with running mascara that gives her face a spider-webbed appearance. She snorts and sucks her breath in with jagged shivers. It is not the subtle kind of crying that others of us have perfected. Impossible to ignore, it causes a Carfagno woman to shove aside her plate and come to us.

"Is this your mother?" the woman asks, sounding accusatory.

I nod.

"Comfort your mother," this woman says. "She's crying." And because the woman is staring at me expectantly, I wrap my arms around my mother's shoulders. I hug her beneath this stranger's approving nod. It is a hollow hug, makeshift, a house-of-cards embrace, and I realize: this is the first time in years we've touched one another. It is not unlike touching something forbidden in a museum, or holding someone else's cat in your lap. Her breath rises and falls, catches, beneath me.

The Carfagno woman pats my shoulder, and I understand she's telling me to move on, away from her family's pavilion with its Budweiser-filled coolers, away from the buffet table with its ambrosia salad.

"There," this woman says, giving me another pat, as if things are this easy, this quick, to mend. "There you go."

"I forgive you, Izzy," my mother says, these words coming out as a shiver. "I do."

Forgiveness is a difficult thing, impossible, the hardest task imaginable.

We try, my mother and I. We take walks around the neighborhood. We rent movies. We eat breakfast Monday mornings at a local diner, she drinking copious amounts of Diet Coke, she sending her eggs back because they have arrived with broken yolks.

"If I wanted broken eggs," my mother has said, "I could have managed that easily at home, free of charge. Really, I'm capable of improperly cooking an egg. Ask my daughter."

"It's okay," I have told the embarrassed waiter. "Really."

Sitting across the table from her, I have deciphered what it is she forgives me for. She forgives me for not being like her; for not fitting easily into this strange, unwieldy world. She forgives me for not cherishing this thing called life she gave me without my asking for it; for loving others better than I have loved her; for avoiding her all these years instead of seeking her out.

I will never tell her that I spent years at attention, waiting for a glimpse of a dirty hat, a red turtleneck, the receding flap of a trench coat. You never know when someone will appear. I looked for him at the Greyhound station as I waited for the bus that would return me to college, and at various diners in downtown Scranton as I drank black coffee and thumbed *The New Yorker*. He might have appeared as I battled the throng of people drinking green beer on the sidelines of the St. Patrick's Day parade; or at the doctor's office as I lay across the table on crumpling, shifting paper, awaiting a proclamation of health; or in the cool, shiny aisles of the supermarket clutching a hunk of disappointing cheese. He might have appeared at my high school graduation, during the uncanny silence that followed the announcement of my name.

Driving east along the highway, I never stopped watching the quickly passing greenery, certain that a man with a red duffel bag would materialize, walking determinedly along the guardrail, anointing the mile markers with perfume as he passed. I had grown very silent by then, but I still had countless things to say to him. *Monsieur, bonjour.* Hello. *Je regrette.* I'm sorry I gave up our secrets. Please say you remember me. I have never forgotten you. *C'est moi*, Belma, beautiful girl, excellent student. Here we are together, again. We're surviving, just as you said we would. Just as you called it.

# PARADISO NEL FRIGORIFERO

Hannah goes into the cooler to talk to the vegetables. When she realizes that it is discriminatory to speak only to the vegetables, she extends conversation to all things: to the plump pink chicken breasts shivering on their melting bed of ice cubes, to the mascarpone and heavy whipping cream, to the pecorino and parmigiano. She addresses the contents of the cooler as a queen addresses her subjects. They shift toward her; she is aware that they listen.

Speaking into the fennel's feathered greenery, she says, "The angel-hair eaters are an obsessive bunch!" To the arugula, its leaves still caked with dirt, "People continue to order cup-of-chinos and expressos. What is chino?" And to the scaloppine, "Antonio's playing Pino Daniele for the fifth time tonight!"

The scaloppine say, "Pino Daniele is a very popular Napoletano singer."

"Like Milli Vanilli," the porcini say. "But Italian and mellower."

The scaloppine say, "Pino Daniele wouldn't be caught dead lip-syncing."

Inside the cooler's thin, artificial air, Hannah announces the specials: "Today, the soup is *piselli e funghi*. The pasta is pasta *mare e monti*. The special entrée is *involtini di manzo con finocchio e mozzarella affumicata*."

"We're not listening," the porcini say. "But we have been told that talking to yourself is a sign of true intelligence. There was a study at an important university."

"Good lord!" the lamb shanks say. "These are pasta and dinner specials, not tragic poems. These are not a hero's epic adventures. No one has died. This isn't school, it's a restaurant!"

"*Thirty days*," begin the porcini, "*hath September, April, June, and November.*"

The vegetables prefer gossip to other exchanges; these vegetables prefer to be in the know.

"We heard that Anna threw a pot at a dishwasher," the escarole says. "Is it true? We heard she asked for fennel and he brought her a funnel."

"Workers drop like flies," say the tomatoes. "How long have you been here?"

"Two months," Hannah says. "Ever since school let out."

"That must be a record," the asparagus says. "The ones before you lasted only days. We've learned that humans often look terrifically ugly when they cry. The servers before you, they hunched inside here and sobbed."

"I'm not crying," Hannah says.

Hannah stands in the cooler in the quiet moments before service; it's the height of summer, and hot everywhere else. She knows the contents of this cooler as intimately as she'd like to know her own skin, knows the particular places Anna stores everything: the old rum bottles filled with chilled coffee for tiramisu, the basil spilling angrily out of its cardboard box, the olives brining in the giant orange barrel, bobbing in their frigid liquid like life rafts on the ocean. Hannah has reached her hand countless times inside this olive barrel, has eaten too many olives, storing their pits inside her palm and studying the sign on the heavy door with its emphatic red lettering: *Push handle! You are not locked inside!*

"Ah, well," the asparagus has said, watching as Hannah digests these words. "I wouldn't be too sure about that."

The vegetables have told her: they find it odd, terribly odd, that Antonio calls her his daughter.

"And *this*," he tells customers who pour him glasses of the wine they've brought, "this beautiful girl is my daughter. A glass, please, for my daughter?" he asks, though Hannah is not legally old enough to drink wine.

These people will believe anything the Italian gentleman says; she and Antonio look nothing alike. He is scarcely old enough to be her father. Frequently, his hand circles her throat, reminding her of the jewelry she doesn't wear as she sips wine that she doesn't like. He has brushed his lips against her ear, has kissed her cheek, residually cold from the cooler.

"Tell him," the broccolini says, "that fathers don't behave like that with their daughters!"

"There are cultural differences," Hannah says.

"Tell him we'd prefer he didn't sing when he comes in here. We are not his audience!"

"He feels us for ripeness," the tomatoes say, "while singing Claudio Villa off-key. It's almost horrific."

The broccolini sings, *"Vieni, c'è una strada nel bosco . . ."*

"He's looking terribly gray," the rosemary says. "This restaurant is taking its toll on him. He was in here earlier, shoving around crates of peppers and mumbling that all of this isn't his dream. It's you and him on the floor, six days a week. He works his other job during the day. It's too much!"

"If it isn't the restaurant," the fennel says, "it's that wife of his! She comes in here and screams because she knows no one can hear her. If she isn't screaming, she's complaining about everybody. She called you *una pecora*. That's a sheep, in case you didn't know."

"You're bilingual?" Hannah asks.

"We're not stupid," the fennel says. "This is basic stuff."

"You're both sheep," the rosemary says. "Together you act like bumbling teenagers around the new cook."

"His name is Anthony," the fennel says. "He makes us swoon."

"He's very good with a knife," says the broccolini. "Unlike the others. They wore their chef's coats like straitjackets! The one before him held eggplant with two hands, as if it was china that might shatter. He cut his finger while chopping cipollini and bled into the mise! A customer found a band-aid in his *sott'olio misto*!"

"*Mi fa schifo*," the fennel says with a shudder.

"Anna threw a colander when she heard about it. Antonio had to grab her arms to settle her. It was like an Italian soap opera!"

"The boy is very good-looking," the zucchini says. "He has what we would call a Roman nose. His forehead is an appropriate size."

"There's nothing Roman about him," the fennel says. "He has an odd midwestern quality. He's the type of mentally unstable man with inflated confidence who'd bungle the intended destruction of a government building."

"*What?*" asks the zucchini.

That night, Hannah recommends the *antipasto di mare* to her tables. She describes its wash of pink and blue and purple hues, the delicate curves of the calamari, the mussels with their sleek black shells, the clams with their almost sandpapery ones. She tells her tables that *frutti di mare*, the Italian word for seafood, translates literally into *fruit from the sea*, something that makes her picture peaches and plums growing in fantastic bunches at the ocean's bottom. She does not cite her source for this information; the scallops told her this one especially sweltering afternoon as Hannah sipped a much-needed Cherry Coke inside the cooler; Anna had just screamed at her for telling a customer, yes, the chef would substitute capellini for fettuccine.

"*Pecora!*" Anna said. "Capellini cannot hold vodka sauce! You are a goat!"

"The *frutti di mare* is a beautiful dish," Hannah tells her tables. "A beautiful, beautiful dish."

"What does that mean?" Customers—usually the men, the unimaginative ones—tend to ask. "What does beautiful *mean?*"

"It's aesthetically pleasing," Hannah says. "It's a lovely dish to look at."

"The point is," a man said on one particular occasion, "I'm not going to sit and stare at it." The men on his right and left laughed heartily. Their laughter mimicked the sound of someone gnawing on corncobs. These are the sorts of men who ask if she expects them to eat the plate when she asks if they are finished.

"Of course," Hannah says. "Of course you're not. The soup is asparagus," she says. "The pasta of the day is *linguini con scoglio* with crabmeat, jumbo shrimp, and fresh cherry tomatoes. The entrée is *costata di agnello*, grilled rack of lamb. The dessert is cheesecake."

Later, as Hannah cuts pastiera for herself, Antonio hovers beside her. His words blow hot air on her cool neck. "You must stop calling it cheesecake," he says.

"It *is* cake and it *is* cheese." The ricotta crumbles like an old building at the edge of her knife.

"When you tell an American *cheesecake*, they think they are getting something with cherries on top. They are assholes in this way." His hand smooths her ribs.

"It looks a little like quiche," she tells her next table under Antonio's sultry gaze. "But it's a dessert. It has ricotta and orange-blossom flavoring. But I want you to know it is not a cheesecake. I want you to understand that it does not have cherries on top." *I want you to know*, she thinks, *that you are not an asshole.*

"There is the question of what to do with you." Antonio slings his arm over her shoulders. He keeps it there often, Hannah has realized, as though the narrow bridge is a shelf. This shelf collapses and his arm surrounds her waist.

"What to do with you," he says again.

"It *is* cheesecake," Hannah tells the roasted peppers, relaxing in their bath of oil. She flicks a thumb at their yellow and red and orange skins, their brown scabs. "For all intents and purposes."

"It isn't quite," the basil says.

"We'd prefer not wasting time on this particular mundane argument," say the peppers. "Cheesecake has a different consistency entirely. But we will say: he shouldn't have pinched you. Geraldo would call that inappropriate touching."

"He's affectionate," says Hannah. "There's something to be said for that."

The cooler door opens, and everything goes hushed. The interior fan moves sluggishly. Anthony stands in the doorway. "Did I disturb you? I thought I heard you talking."

"No." Hannah watches dumbly as he fills a plastic container with steady handfuls of reggiano. She says, "Talking to yourself is a sign of intelligence. They did a study at an important university."

"I'll remember that," he says.

"These things are good for surviving uncomfortable moments," she says. "These tiny facts."

"Right," he says.

"I hear you're very good with a knife."

"I am," he says, clutching his container of reggiano, "very good with a knife."

"Do you love cooking?" Hannah asks.

He shrugs.

"That boy," the baccalà says when he is gone. "We don't like him."

"That's ridiculous," Hannah says.

"Not ridiculous," the baccalà says.

"He's Virgo," say the peppers. "We've learned not to trust Virgo men. We find they're creative individuals who often have problems communicating their emotions effectively. They tend to be emotionally challenged and far too critical. You're Scorpio, and too much of an emotional wreck for Virgo."

"He's very unhappy," the baccalà says. "Yesterday, he kicked over a crate of tomatoes. He punched a hole in a box of lemons. We've heard him out there, throwing things when they don't work properly. He has what we call anger management issues. And it isn't natural that he never talks about himself. You people are always talking about yourselves. We're subjected to your constant weepy monologues: this is wrong, and this and that and *oh my God*. You bite your lips and your cheeks and ask *why, why, why?* Once a girl dried her eyes with the basil."

"Who are you to judge?" Hannah asks, and wonders if the baccalà will notice her tone. She's afraid it might interrogate her: why this sharp voice? She doesn't want to explain herself to a fish. She wants to tell it, instead, about its poor reputation, how people believe she's talking about a dried, salted fish when she mentions its name, how people twist their mouths a particular way when they pronounce baccalà. They ask for salmon and halibut and, in acute moments of desperation, grouper and tilapia; they prefer the bottom feeders to baccalà.

"I find him very polite," she says. "Always nice."

"Ha!" the baccalà says, louder and more arrogantly than Hannah has ever heard baccalà speak.

Anthony and Hannah share *spaghetti al pomodoro* and *melanzane a funghetto* and *sott'olio misto* and *scarola saltata* and *misto di ortaggi* and *gemelli al pesto* while Pino Daniele plays on the CD player, and Hannah is reminded of something somebody once told her: Pino Daniele is a popular Napoletano musician, though she can't remember who told her this.

She says, "Pino Daniele is a great Napoletano musician." From across the room, Anna watches them as she adds the night's sales, drinks her second, her third, glass of wine.

Anthony speaks around a mouthful of escarole. "I think he sucks."

"Why don't you ever talk about yourself?"

"What is there to say?"

"Come on," Hannah says.

"I slice eggplant. I mince garlic. Sometimes, when the dishwasher is sick, I wash dishes, and I'm careful to rinse and sanitize."

"That isn't what I mean," Hannah says.

"I don't know anything worth saying," he says. "I'm twenty-four. I live in Pittsburgh."

"That isn't it, either." She wishes herself capable of mitigating silence, taking it firmly between two palms. She wants to hold it above her head like something to be smashed against a block of concrete. She says, "It takes three weeks for a banana peel to decompose."

He says, "I hate bananas."

"Potassium is essential for healthy living," Hannah says.

"I'm saving money," he says after a moment. "I want to get the hell out of here, go to France or Italy. Anna has family in Naples. She said I could stay with them. Or maybe Croatia. Maybe Switzerland. I can go anywhere, really. I can do whatever I want."

"You can," Hannah says.

They share zuppetta napoletana.

"Watch Antonio," Anthony says. "Some people, you can't trust."

"The cream in the zuppetta tastes weird." Hannah spreads powdered sugar with the tip of her knife, building it into small piles that she crushes to avoid looking at him.

"I'm just saying," he says.

Anna makes the desserts herself: *zuppetta*, with its layers of puff pastry and pastry cream and soaked sponge cake; *torta di bosco*, cake of the woods, with its chantilly cream and its top studded with berries; *pastiera*, Hannah's favorite, the cheesecake that is not a cheesecake with its cooked grain and ricotta and orange-blossom water, served especially, Anna says, for Easter holiday; *tiramisu*, which Anna serves only because the American sheep demand it. She is teaching Anthony the art of these pastries, this discourse of cream and filling, this whipping and folding.

"Do you know?" the pignoli ask. "Anna was explaining about the grain in the pastiera, and when she touched his shoulder to get his attention, he threw her hand down and told her he wasn't in the fucking mood for this shit!"

"Everyone has bad days," Hannah says.

"*You* are the sheep," the pignoli say.

The ricotta says, "He touched her angrily and then stormed away. We were forced to sit out for a long time, getting warm."

"I have never seen him behave like that," Hannah says.

"That is because you are not intimate with him."

"What do you mean, intimate?" Hannah asks, but the ricotta has said its piece.

That night, as the Pino Daniele CD begins its third rotation of the evening, two scaloppine meant for table twelve disappear from the kitchen window.

"Where are they?" Anna demands, arms bent at her waist.

"What?" Hannah clips an order to the metal rack.

"The scaloppine," Anna says. "You took them. I saw you."

"I didn't."

"*Bugiarda!*" Anna says. "Female hands took them! And those hands were not mine. I cooked those scaloppine. All you do is carry them. Badly! You walk too quickly and tilt the plate and sauce spills onto its lip. Don't think I haven't seen it! I have respect for the things I make, if you don't!" She moves to the dish room, hands fluttering in the direction of the sink. "And Ahmed. The dishwasher who never changes dishwater." Reaching deep, she releases the dishwater. Down it goes with a steady gargling sound, and when the water has disappeared down the drain, every last drop, there are the two scaloppine, pale and bloated, on the sink's silver bottom. Anna pulls out a single piece. She holds it up for all to inspect before dropping it back with a loud slap and calling for Antonio.

"Look at that," Antonio says. "Scaloppine in the sink." He appears amused by the sound of it.

"She took them," Anna says, pointing at Hannah. "She put them in the sink! I saw her!"

"I did not," Hannah says, and inside her stomach, something moves. She has never before been indicted in a lie.

"I saw her," Anna says. "With my own eyes."

"Of course she didn't," Antonio says, pinching Hannah's cheek. He drags a finger along the line of her chin, and Anna throws a spatula, clattering, across the dish room's tiled floor.

"You defend her!" Anna says, hoisting a fry pan.

"This is ridiculous," Anthony interrupts, appearing in the doorway between the kitchen and the dish room. He has said nothing until now, concentrating instead on the grill, turning the shrimp, patiently blackening their sides. He has been cooking sausage, watching its skin wrinkle and pull like an old man's.

"*I* say what's ridiculous," Anna says. "You cook the shrimp."

"You forget that I don't have to cook anything," he says. "If I don't want to."

Anna's silence is sudden, like an apple falling from a tree; like a rock falling toward a car's window.

For the rest of the night, whenever she slips a plate of scaloppine in the window, she leans toward Hannah and says, "I see you, now,

taking that. You see her taking that, too. We see you, both of us,"
Anna says, while Anthony chops onion without crying, refuses to
look up.

"An apology," Antonio says, offering Hannah a slice of mimosa
cake when this terrible night is finally over. "For Anna. *Pazzissima*."

Hannah shoves the lemon garnish into her mouth.

"You are a good girl," Antonio says, watching Hannah chew. "You
are a nice girl, but you hide your attraction." He touches her sweater
sleeve. "For instance, this. You look like a grandmother."

"This is my favorite sweater," Hannah says, suddenly sick with
lemon.

"You see." Antonio's arm settles on her shoulders. "You're young,
and you'll want to fuck. But who'll fuck a girl wearing a sweater like
this?" His hand rubs her cheek. The scent of wine quivers on his
breath. "I'll forgive the sweater if you tell me: are you a virgin?"

"This cake tastes like paper-mache," Hannah says.

"There is only one thing I need right now. You can help me with
that. Anna is too busy teaching that boy to make cakes and whatever else. She thinks I don't notice, but really, I don't care. There is
a distinction."

"Is there another slice of this?" Hannah asks around heavy forkfuls.

"You'll gain weight," Antonio tells her. "And then you'll be a cow,
wearing an ugly sweater. No, you shouldn't eat that." His fingers rest
on the rim of the plate as delicately as the flowers painted there.

"You brought it to me," Hannah says, "to eat."

Antonio shrugs.

"I like this sweater. I *like* cows."

"Such patient, stupid animals," Antonio says. And then he is gone,
whisking the plate away.

The buffalo mozzarella wants to know how she can allow anyone
to speak to her like that.

"Seriously!" the pignoli say, voices muffled behind plastic.

"And that stunt Anna pulled," the escarole says. "Like *that* wasn't terribly contrived! Did that crazy woman think she was fooling anyone?"

"Speak to your mother," the zucchini says. "She'll tell you that you should have spoken up, set him straight."

Hannah doesn't usually listen to the zucchini, because whenever she eats it, she gets sick. She once stayed up the entire night, vomiting, after she'd eaten the smallest bit. She does not consider it a reliable vegetable. She looks to the tomatoes for their esteemed opinion.

"We agree," the tomatoes say. "You should definitely talk to her."

Nights after work, Hannah stays up with her mother watching reruns of her mother's favorite trivia game show. Her mother is never concerned with answering the questions correctly; she only wants to answer them faster than the show's contestants do.

Tonight the host says, "An arboreal mammal also called a honey bear."

"Ostrich!" Hannah's mother answers.

"My boss says weird things to me sometimes," Hannah says.

"Like what?" her mother blinks up from the television set.

"The other day, he suggested I was unattractive."

"You could wear makeup," her mother says. "You could pluck your eyebrows. You're old enough to understand that women at least need to try, Hannah."

The host leans into his sliver of a microphone and reads from his card, "A large voracious marine fish."

"Squid!" her mother answers.

"He says other things," Hannah says. "He says a lot of things."

"That's just it." Her mother leans across the coffee table for a cigarette. "People say things to people, don't they?" She flicks a match efficiently. "It's called conversation."

A girl calls for Anthony. Hannah answers the phone, balancing plates, shifting them.

"I'm busy," he says when Hannah tells him. He pours a steady stream of oil into a pan of escarole, the oil swishing anxiously against the sides of the bottle when he sets it on the counter.

"He's busy," Hannah says into the receiver.

"It's important," the girl says, and her voice sounds puffy. "I've been trying to reach him for days, now."

"It's important, she says."

"*This* is important." He moves the pan on the burner, and Hannah imagines the raisins growing fatter in the oil.

"It's a girl," Hannah says.

"I know who it is. I'm fucking busy." Pans clatter and shuffle. Anna glares at her over minced garlic, and when Hannah returns to the phone, the girl has hung up.

"Thank you, Hannah," Anthony says, touching the *pollo pulcinella* with his index finger to see if it is finished cooking. "Thank you."

In the cooler, the artichokes bristle. "We're not sure about this Anthony fellow," they say.

She tells them, "He's never overcooked a scaloppine. His panzerotti are perfectly golden. His pasta is al dente. There are never complaints. People point to the kitchen and say, *What a handsome chef!* They want to know, *Is he classically trained?*"

"We all know the answer to that," the artichokes say.

"Don't be snarky," Hannah says.

"We're talking about his personality. We think you're interested in him. Let us tell you: it's a very bad idea."

"Some people aren't interested in anything," Hannah says.

The artichokes say, "It seems you've gotten defensive, recently."

"What do you know about defenses?" Hannah plucks an artichoke leaf.

"We think you're weak," the artichokes say. "This woman who called. He didn't even have the dignity to speak to her!"

"What do artichokes know about dignity?" Hannah asks, and does not tell them there were seven hang-ups after the first call. She counted. Hannah is certain it was the girl with the puffy voice, though she did not tell Anthony.

The artichokes ask, "What does a girl know about anything?"

✻   ✻   ✻

Anthony prepares *insalata tricolore*, careful to choose the nicest pieces of radicchio and endive, of arugula. He tells Hannah, "Greens lose their flavor when they're kept too cold."

"See, you know that," Hannah says.

"I don't. Anna told me."

"Most shark attacks aren't fatal," Hannah says. "Most are bites."

"It doesn't matter," he says. "I've never been to the ocean. The closest I've come to water is one of those dirty rivers."

"Who was that girl?"

"What girl?"

"On the phone."

"My sister," he says, and Hannah understands he is lying. "She calls at the worst times."

At the end of the night, Claudio Villa sings. Hannah and Anthony share saltimbocca under Anna's watchful eye and Hannah says, "Saltimbocca means *jumps in the mouth*, literally."

"I'll drive you home," he says.

His car carries the unnatural scent of winter and pine needles despite the summer heat. Shadows fold across their faces as they pass beneath street lamps. He gnaws thoughtfully on his bottom lip.

"Is something wrong?" Hannah asks when they reach her house.

"Besides everything?"

"Oh," Hannah says.

He says, "In this car, if you searched the cushions, there would be forty dollars, at least. Maybe fifty. Shall we?"

For the quickest moment she allows *shall we* to mean anything, everything, and then she understands he means the car seats. He means the hidden nickels, dimes, and pennies lost between the curves of stained velour. Together, they squeeze their hands between cushions. The interior light is broken, and they grope in the dark, the headlights of passing cars occasionally glinting, tossing bright shapes on their shoulders and backs. Twice, they bump heads and Hannah laughs nervously. She dislodges from the cushions stale crumbs, a handful of quarters and dimes, two ink pens, several small bent straws she associates with juice boxes, a woman's vintage rhinestone barrette. She says nothing about the barrette, clutching it instead inside her sweaty palm as if she hasn't found it.

"Do you want to come in?" Hannah asks. "There's hot chocolate."

"It's ninety degrees out," he says. "A heat wave."

"Ice water?"

"No, thank you."

"I guess I'll see you tomorrow," Hannah says.

"Right." He looks at her as if she's just asked him to solve an impossible mathematic equation.

"What?"

"Nothing," he says. "Never mind."

His car, when it pulls away, sounds hungry, nearly angry. It sucks up gas until it is gone, out of sight.

"Anthony didn't show today," the buffalo mozzarella says when Hannah enters the cooler.

"No call, no show," says the rapini. "Anna was frantic! On the edge of tears. She threw an iced tea bottle and then shouted obscenities when it didn't break!"

"I am so tired," the buffalo mozzarella says, "of people throwing things around here!"

"People get sick," Hannah says. "They have hundred-and-five-degree fevers. Their cars sometimes refuse to start."

"Something isn't right," the buffalo mozzarella says. "I have a mother's intuition. Last night I dreamt that a girl stood perilously close to a lake."

"Did she not know how to swim?" Hannah asks. "Was it very deep? I don't see the inherent problem in standing beside a lake."

"People drown in bathtubs, Hannah," the rapini interjects. "Babies die sleeping in cribs."

"I woke up before the end," says the buffalo mozzarella, "but I intuited a dreadful accident. She didn't look like you. This girl must have blown her hair out with a rounded brush. She must have used expensive products. Her hair was so much smoother than yours. It might not have been you."

"Everything was fine when he drove me home," Hannah says.

"He drove you home!" the rapini says. "Probably you waited like a fool in the moonlight for him to kiss you! He's seven years your senior!"

The buffalo mozzarella says, "She's not his *sister*. What do you make of *that*?"

"When did you begin speaking in italics?" Hannah asks the buffalo mozzarella.

For the rest of the night, the contents of the cooler will not speak to her. The vegetables grow silent when she steps inside for a moment's rest. The castelvetrano olives toss fitfully inside their brine.

"Polyethylene was discovered by accident," she tells a solitary chicken breast, fingering the pink flesh beneath its wrapper, and the chicken, despite its solitude, refuses to answer.

"You're touching raw chicken!" the buffalo mozzarella abandons its silence long enough to say. "Use your brain, Hannah! Consider salmonella!"

She cradles the lemons carefully inside her palms, and they, too, will not speak to her. She turns them over and under, holds them beside her ear, and hears only silence. Hannah is reminded of grade school and certain days when girls would not speak to her on the playground because they did not like her shoes, her hair, her socks, the way she gnawed the inside of her cheek, the picture on her folder, the way she held her pencil. In third grade, certain mean girls held up pictures of rhinoceroses in the *Encyclopedia Britannica,* comparing them to her, but acknowledging that perhaps even they were more attractive.

When Anthony is not at work a second day, Anna hands Hannah a chef's knife.

"You'll have to mince," Anna says. "That one is useless," she says, motioning toward Antonio, who reads his newspaper, drinks his coffee. He hums something that Hannah identifies as a Pino Daniele song. "Good for Nothing."

Hannah never knew she could mince. And yet she minces, rocking the chef's knife gently over garlic, watching as the pieces become smaller. Her pieces are small but not uniform, imperfect. She is still mincing when Anna lifts her own cutting board from the counter, throws it loudly against the floor. Cipolline roll to and fro beneath the prep table.

"Now, what good is a cutting board on the floor?" Antonio asks, pushing aside his newspaper and coming to Anna. "Onions on the floor won't bring him back."

His hand alights momentarily on her neck before she bats it away.

The cook hired to take Anthony's place is overweight. The elastic band of his chef's pants barely contain his stomach; his pants drop down disconcertingly. He constantly shoves things in his mouth without washing his hands: the folded skins of roasted peppers, hunks of Parmesan, handfuls of pignoli. He gnaws at tomatoes and fennel bulbs as if they are peaches. Hannah has seen his chin glistening with juice.

"You are fat and dumb!" Anna says when she discovers him hunched inside the cooler, eating slices of bacon she'd cooked for the night's carbonara special.

"Come, now," Antonio says. "Come. They can't all be Anthony."

On his fourth day, the new cook calls in sick because he cannot locate his wallet, and Hannah listens as Anna screams into the phone, stretching the cord across the kitchen as she slices eggplant. "That makes no sense! What you are saying makes no sense! You are not sick because your wallet is missing! What, did you accidentally eat it?"

"Things fall apart," the tomatoes say. It is mid-August, the height of summer, and the tomatoes are no longer mundane cherry and plum, but heirloom, their skins speckled and beautiful, marbled greens and reds and yellows that remind Hannah of a glass pane inside a church window. The tomatoes do not say this to Hannah. They no longer speak to her, but murmur disapprovingly among themselves.

"They'll be fine," she says, and the tomatoes answer, "We weren't actually talking to you."

She is surprised, then, when two weeks later the tomatoes address her directly. "Have you heard?" they ask when she enters the cooler.

"Heard what?" Hannah expects some gossip about the new cook:

he called in sick after losing his keys; he sliced off the tip of his index finger while chopping zucchini; he was found sitting on a crate of lettuces, licking a stick of butter like a hard candy.

"The rumor," the eggplant says, "is that he killed her. With a what-do-you-call-it?"

"A machete," the reggiano says. "And it's no longer a rumor when it's printed in the paper."

"Not true," says the eggplant.

"What?" Hannah asks.

"It's a knife," the eggplant says. "Like something someone would use thwacking brush in the jungle. It's the kind of thing that appears handily in made-for-television movies when the protagonist is lost in a remote place. *Oh, look, let's use this machete!*"

"*Machete* is a Spanish word," says the reggiano. "A diminutive of *macho.*"

"He was macho!" the eggplant says. "He bludgeoned her in their bed."

"Who?" Hannah asks.

"The boy," the zucchini says. "We're talking about the boy."

"Anthony," the eggplant says.

The reggiano adds, "You kept saying he had good knife skills!"

"Human emotions continue to elude me," the zucchini says. "Just when I thought the only act any of you were truly capable of was weeping dramatically inside the cooler and feeling sorry for yourselves."

"He killed his girlfriend," the zucchini says. "The mother of his child. The child is a girl. She's only two! She was in the next room!"

"Anna cried when she heard," the reggiano says. "*She wept*, like Jesus."

"It was rather ungainly," the eggplant says. "She looked like a horse eating too many carrot sticks at once. Or like someone had stretched her jaw out, like people stretch out their fancy leather shoes with those what-do-you-call-them."

"They're called shoehorns," the reggiano says.

"She looked like she had swallowed a shoehorn," says the eggplant.

Hannah says, "Please excuse me."

"I wouldn't go up there," the zucchini says. "They've been at it all morning. It's like a scene from *Being Bobby Brown*, but less civil."

Nothing had been amiss when Hannah passed through the dining room on her way to the cooler. The room had been quiet, arranged as she'd left it the night before, the tables set for dinner service, napkins folded, silverware buffed—forks to the left, knives to the right, water glass to the right, wine glass to the left. Hannah finds Anna draped over table five, the settings pushed aside, her forehead pressed into the cloth. She holds fistfuls of fettucine, weeps. Strewn across the floor is every variety of dry pasta imaginable: spaghetti, gemelli, rigatoni, farfalle, fettucine, penne. Antonio leans against the wall, his head angled beside a painting depicting pastel sailboats docked in the Bay of Naples. He smokes a cigarette with his eyes closed, as if to will himself away from this unfortunate scene. His lids flutter open when Hannah appears.

"Oh," he says when he sees her, surprised by her presence. And then he is putting the cigarette out, mustering himself to go to Anna. He leans close, whispers in Anna's ear something that Hannah is not meant to hear but hears. "Don't embarrass me," he says. "The girl is watching you. Wipe your face."

And then he is wrapping his arms around Anna in what Hannah guesses is a display of solidarity, but his touch undoes her. Anna screams in the manner that Hannah imagines the girl bludgeoned inside her bed screamed. It's possibly the longest scream Hannah has ever heard; it sounds like the screams of countless horror movies spliced together. *Healthy set of lungs on her*, Hannah imagines the tomatoes saying. *Crazy bitch*, the asparagus might say. Ahmed runs out of the dish room holding a skillet.

"*Cosa?*" Antonio asks. He pulls away from her, gesticulates madly.

"I hate you," Anna says. "You disgust me. Your touch makes vomit crawl inside my throat every single time."

And then, undoing her apron, she stalks out of the room.

"This place," Antonio says when Anna is gone. He has turned on Pino Daniele, retrieved the broom from the closet. He sounds more tired than Hannah has ever heard him. "It is a fucking mess."

"Oh," Hannah says, if only to take up space.

And then he is walking toward her, taking her face and squashing it like an overripe plum between his large palms. She feels his hot bitter breath, and then he is pressing his dry lips against her own. It takes Hannah a moment to realize that this thing he does is meant to be kissing. She clamps her mouth tightly shut, makes it a fortress, a wall around a city a person is forbidden entrance to, and when he realizes that he has been denied this entrance, he takes her entire head roughly in both hands and shoves it aside like someone's meddlesome cat.

"You know where the broom is," he says, nudging his chin toward the pasta-strewn floor. "You know how to use it."

That night, Hannah sees Anthony on the evening news. Her mother has ordered chicken wings, and he appears on the six o'clock telecast as her mother wipes ranch from the corners of her lips with a dishtowel.

"I heard about this guy," her mother says around a mouthful of chicken. "Someone mentioned this at work. A machete! The baby was in the next room!"

He appears on the television screen, washed-out and already thinner, the camera jostling as he is led to the police car at the edge of the frame, his face averted so that Hannah sees only his chin, sharp as a paper cut. The reporter has just asked him a question, several questions, and he throws his response casually over his shoulder.

"I refuse to answer," he says. "Talking is a sign of intelligence." He dips beneath a sea of clamoring hands, the police car's door closing behind him.

"Talking is a sign of intelligence!" Hannah's mother nearly chokes on her wing. "Ha!"

Hannah feels the quick pinch of disappointment: he has not even gotten this right. Some people are determined not to get things right. In this way, she learns that nothing surprises her. When she sees Anna nearly a year later, Hannah knows this with certitude. Anna stands outside the restaurant in the thick August heat, chastising the red-faced delivery driver over some unacceptable porcini mushrooms, her hands resting on her pregnant stomach, protecting it, even as she berates this man. Hannah raises her own hand, gestures to Anna hello, and in the simmering heat, Anna squints back at her, pretends to decipher who the hell Hannah is, before turning her head and her stomach away.

These things do not surprise her.

Their last exchange occurred soon after Hannah refused the broom Antonio offered her and went instead to say goodbye to the vegetables. She discovered Anna already inside the cooler. She'd turned off the interior light and was sitting on a crate of radicchio, smoking in the darkness, silencing the vegetables around her. The ember at the end of her cigarette swelled, died, bloomed again. She drank from a chilled bottle of rum, which she offered to Hannah, who refused it.

"It is a paradise here," Anna said as the fan whirred, "inside this refrigerator. Very cool and silent. A person can think here. A person can *breathe*. Do you know, where we come from is called the Campi Flegrei, but I have also heard it called the mouth of hell. It is the mythological home of the Roman god of fire, Vulcan. Do you know him?" She did not wait for Hannah's response. "Antonio and I drove to a place named California not far from here, a place named California, Pennsylvania, where there is a university with a statue of Vulcan, and we stood underneath his hammer and touched it, and I understood that this, actually, is the mouth of hell, though Antonio is too dumb to know it. Do you know," she said, inhaling deeply on her cigarette, "that the word in this case is the same in both English and Italian. It is called machete in both cases."

They sat together, growing cold. Hannah heard the basil shiver and sigh.

"You are too young to understand," Anna said, exhaling. "But for sure, the mouth of hell is in Pennsylvania. Who knew? Who would ever guess such a thing?"

And then, because she was not actually surprised, Hannah shrugged.

# AMERICAN SILK

Stevie was a good worker, a good man, and his greatest crime—or so Deb and I would have guessed—was only that he was slightly *off*, like chartreuse yarn muddled in the dye process, or a quart of souring milk. At the bar, drinking up the watered down drinks of happy hour, Deb claimed a man got like that when he turned forty without a wife and family to place him at the head of the dining table, to declare him king of things. A man went irrefutably south when he did not have invasive weeds to vanquish, a riding lawnmower to straddle. He needed the comfortable easy chair and the changeability of the television channels, the tilting of deferential heads toward him, not unlike the laying down of palms, the parting of crowds. Without these things a man simply languished, like something left too long in the heat.

"It's true," Deb said. She sipped her drink with the feigned hesitance of a person who prefers you don't notice how many drinks she's drinking. "A man needs a family to build his confidence. He needs a woman. He needs children, or else he gets insecure. Look at Mitch."

Mitch was Deb's husband. I'd never met him, had only seen pictures. He didn't seem like a man who needed even an extra drop of confidence. He had killed a buck the past hunting season, and Deb had pinned the crimped picture, husband and buck, to the board beside her desk. Mitch hovered thick-necked and broad-shouldered in the foreground, smiling in the infuriating way of dumb men, a smile so squat and broad it gave his eyes the appearance of conflict, as if each eye wanted to veer in opposite directions and had yet to resolve this issue. He nudged the deer's face to the camera as if he were nudging the face of a drunken and inept friend who'd stripped down to his underwear and whose picture had to be snapped in this moment of humiliation and defeat.

"Mitch is complicated," Deb said.

"A Renaissance man," I imagined saying, but did not.

They had been a couple since their freshman year of high school, had wed immediately after college, and had been married now for ten years. Still, Deb admitted as she furiously sucked the last drops of her fuzzy navel: even *she*, a happily married woman, could not deny her weakness for Stevie. Stevie was attractive, she said, the way socially inept men are always attractive. Midafternoon, when the three of us had the subtle sheen of sweat on our necks and faces, Stevie skirted the corners of the aisles with the dolly, balancing a box of Magenta or Lavender, and Deb would yearn to touch his biceps, as beautiful and clearly defined as an anatomy lesson.

"Stevie's a freak," I said, for Stevie always rose with a startled look when I spoke to him, when I asked him for something as simple as a cone of Maple. He ate his lunches alone, and these lunches were always the stiff, processed lunches of a depressed person. He drank coffee dispensed from the downstairs vending machine, and the tiny paper cups sat like small distressed white birds inside his large palm. He'd attended the Memorial Day picnic with his good friend, William Coon, whom Deb tried desperately to make conversation with (*What is it you do, William; how long have you known Stevie?*), but rather than speaking, William Coon preferred stuffing strawberries into his mouth, the tops collecting in an unnervingly large pile. Even his last name, Coon, seemed like something he had killed and attached to a board with pins. He and Stevie wore flannel despite the blistering heat; Stevie spent the entire afternoon whittling something ambiguous from a discarded stick. Stevie had always demonstrated great prowess with the X-Acto knife, slicing open boxes with more relish than he showed doing anything else, and it should not have been surprising, then, when the supervisor informed us on a Monday morning, mid-June, weeks after Deb admitted her infatuation: Stevie's good friend William Coon had killed his girlfriend, and Stevie had been an accomplice in this murder. William Coon had used a machete, hacking the girlfriend's body into bits, and Stevie had thrown the severed pieces into the Susquehanna River.

"We *knew* this man," the supervisor said, giving the slight, effeminate shiver of condescension he was so fond of. "We *worked* with him."

"It wasn't Stevie," Deb said.

"It was Stevie," the supervisor said.

"It couldn't have been." She coddled two cones of Cardinal to her chest. Her voice had a tired, hypnotic lull, like waves lapping against the side of something.

"Stevie was a freak," I said. "He had sublimated anger."

"He wasn't a murderous freak."

"But he was," I said.

"We had drinks," she told me later, at the bar. "We had conversation." Sitting there, bent over the various rocks glasses strewn about the table, the severity of her beauty struck me. Her purple halter appeared shocking against her skin. She looked ethereal, like blown glass. She had the classic beauty, I noted, that evoked man's betrayal. She might one day disappear in a boating accident, or begin a tumultuous relationship with the president.

"You had conversation. With *Stevie*? When did you do such a thing?"

"He took pieces of a woman's body," she said, "and threw them into a river. You think you know someone until you realize they own a machete and they don't mind the literal handling of dead flesh." Her voice, typically heavy with mustered enthusiasm, held the tick of sarcasm.

"It was his friend's machete," I said. "It may not have been the *direct* handling of flesh. He could have worn gloves."

"Whatever," she said. Her cheeks had a drunken pink sheen. "You never actually know a person. You think you have a clue about them; you think you understand them. It's useless."

"Don't be so maudlin."

"Maudlin!" she scoffed, voice sharp. "Where'd you get *that*?" Her arm swung up, motioning for another drink. "Maudlin!"

Hovered over my own drink, I did not understand her surprise. This was not an unexpected kink in Stevie's life but a logical progression. Some things never made any sense, but others achieved a final startling clarity, an abrupt halo of light. As my father once told me, waxing poetic over too much Scotch: nothing stayed boiling beneath the surface. If a person punched something down over *there*, it was, certainly, going to come up over *here*.

We worked in a textile mill that manufactured furniture upholstery—lovely fern- and salmon-colored silk for upper-class sofas; intimidating gold- and cardinal-threaded jacquards for hotel banquettes; bold, abrasive stripes for middle-class couches. The supervisor was a friend of my father's and had hired me as a yarn clerk the summer between my junior and senior years of college. I had wanted to work in the office, with the thrum of the air-conditioning, the comforting lull of the office machinery. I had wanted the assurance of the alphabetical files, the regulatory pluck of the Muzak, but was hired, instead, by the yarn department to sort cones of yarn. These cones came up each morning on the freight elevator—ten, twelve, thirteen boxes of cones I sorted according to weight and color and dye lot, shoving them back in the boxes they'd come from. Minutes later Stevie plucked them back out—if Stevie did such a thing as pluck—to send to weaving. The yarn department was, according to the supervisor, perennially short-handed and desperate. Apparently, no one reliable wished to sort yarn for a living.

"Office machinery is a bitch, Emma," my mother said when I complained about this. "You're too much of a naïve, inexperienced lamb to cope with the nightmare of a paper jam or a facsimile problem. You don't have the self-confidence, the certitude, to deal with the secretary's neuroses."

My father said, "I hope you're sorting carefully," concerned, as usual, when his reputation was at stake.

"Like a pro," I said.

"Don't go saying what you make," he said. "If anyone asks."

Deb was the supervisor's *liaison*, the person immediately responsible for our department. She grappled daily with mundane things: a shipment of Cardinal that had not been received, an order sent to weaving mistakenly filled with Ash rather than Dust. She was responsible for hiring Stevie's replacement, but she'd found no one except a man who'd shown up for his interview with the same withered look as Stevie, suggesting he, too, might kill a person. The supervisor clucked about, nervous that no one had been hired. And then, he announced: he'd found a replacement himself. Michael Rodney, formerly of weaving, would be transferred to our department *pronto.*

"I thought he got *fired* from weaving," Deb said. "How can he be transferred if he was *fired?*"

"He got *un*fired," the supervisor said. "He has a family to support. He has kids. He came to me and talked to me and asked me for this job. He showed initiative."

"It isn't that," Deb said. Her voice had the same scoffing tone I'd heard at the bar. "It isn't initiative. That man is incapable of showing initiative. We're not desperate."

"We're desperate," the supervisor clarified.

"Not that desperate," Deb said.

Michael Rodney rolled into work late that first day, deeply tanned and leathery. The various parts of his body crackled with a vibrant athleticism, a masculinity. His gait, even his posture, implied that things were susceptible to disaster when men were not near. He was a man you'd want to lug you somewhere with the hope of teaching you something, a man whose sweat you'd consider tasting with a sensitive, darting tongue. He had good bone structure, a handsome mouth. A person looked at him, and looked twice. He gave the impression that he knew this.

He said, "*Deborah.*"

She said, "*Michael.* You're late."

"Yeah, well."

"Generally, here in the yarn department, we come to work when we're asked."

"Of course, absolutely." In Michael Rodney's voice, statements lost their absolute quality. They gained, instead, a fledgling ambiguity, became things that could be flung aside with an emphatic shake. His voice made the seeming simplicity of syllables disconcerting. "*Absolutely.*"

Michael Rodney held his unwavering, lazy bravado not close to his chest but unfurled like a giant umbrella, bountifully colored, though his nervous habits gave him away: the persistent action of his foot, tapping, the cyclical movement of tobacco finding its way inside his mouth. He started on a Monday and did not speak to me for two days, staring in silence over boxes of Ivory and Lemongrass as he filled orders to be sent to weaving. His steady look was one of disdain, as if I'd done something terrible to him and failed to be accountable for it.

"Where we are," he said the third day, as if this silence had been too much for him, had demanded a self-restraint he simply couldn't muster; he would deign to speak even to me, "time fucking stops. It doesn't move. This place is purgatory for losers. What's your excuse?"

"I'm being forced to."

"Your parents are making you work!" he said.

"And anyway, I'm leaving at the end of August."

"So you're better than the rest of us because you're leaving?"

"Right, that's exactly what I said."

"How does a girl like you get hired for a job like this? Oh, right," he answered himself. "Don't worry, I won't ask what your starting wages are."

"Good."

"What's a girl like you study in college?"

"English."

"Useful," he said with that perfected irony.

"We do speak it."

"Oh, right." He paused. "So, smart girl, what was your opinion on Stevie?"

"He was a freak. I'm not surprised."

"I mean, was he handsome? Would you have slept with him?"

"That question," I said, "constitutes sexual harassment."

"Someone who thinks they're very smart would call it that." He shrugged, kicked at the dusty ground.

"He was dangerously attractive," I said. "Now he's just dangerous." I was aware, as soon as I'd said it, of the inanity of this statement.

"Very insightful," Michael Rodney said. "Poetic, even. I see that you're incredible. Brilliant, in fact."

"Thanks," I said.

"You're welcome."

He preferred his last name, Rodney, as if he considered himself distinct enough not to need the superfluity of a first name. I'd learned already, in my twenty-one years, that a man who went by his last name was a strange breed, not to be trusted, prone to ridiculous kinds of rage, stuffed full of inflated ego. Michael Rodney was no exception. He epitomized the brand of anger I'd seen on late-night made-for-TV movies, and talk shows regarding the outcome of paternal testing—the kind of anger I'd never, in the life I'd lived, been exposed to, but which I'd always had a curiosity about. This anger flared up continually, feeding on the air's oppressive humidity.

"I didn't even go to college," Rodney said, unsolicited, one afternoon. "I didn't even apply." We were sorting cones in the back of the department, fourth aisle, where the final letters of the alphabet were stashed: Violet, Watermelon, and Yellow. Someone had slid several boxes of Pale Yellow into place beside Yellow, and this inconsistency annoyed me. Beyond us, the industrial sized fans whirred, keeping the beat to something indiscernible. "I'm still here."

"There's nothing wrong with it."

"Did I fucking say there was? Did I say that?"

"No—."

"Then what's your fucking point?"

That same afternoon, he tossed the roaches running violently at the bottom of what was once a box filled with Ruby over the edge of the fire escape. Roaches flew through the air like a small, brief plague, like brown indiscriminate warnings, and the women at the decaying picnic table below, eating their lunches, jumped up, frantically brushing their shoulders and the napes of their necks. They shielded their eyes against the sun and screamed up to him, "Rodney! You asshole!"

Leaning against the fire escape's rusty railing, he asked, "Yeah, *so?*"

Deb was far away in the supervisor's office on this occasion of the flung roaches, unavailable to provide mitigation or mediation, the sorts of things the person in charge usually provides. The supervisor had, soon after Michael Rodney's arrival, left for Italy on a two-week jaunt, riding on an air-conditioned bus with other culturally weary middle-aged American travelers, seeing the things they thought they should see in a lifetime, checking them off like a grocery list. He was stuffing himself with polpette and carbonara while Deb passed the time in his office. Rodney took this opportunity to rifle Deb's desk drawers, opening and closing them, paging through dog-eared files, crumpling papers. Nothing personal and noteworthy revealed itself, though in the top left drawer she kept several jars of nail polish, all shades of violent red, which Rodney pocketed, along with two haggard-looking lipsticks and the picture of Mitch and his dull-eyed buck.

"For my wife," he said, holding up the lipsticks.

"And the picture?"

"For me," he said. "This is a handsome man, a handsome buck, don't you think? Mitchell was a *hero* to catch this buck."

"Three cheers for our hero, Mitch," I said.

"*Exactly,*" Rodney said. He shifted his weight. "But where's our fearless leader? We need authority around here, guidance. We need supervision. It's what she gets paid for. She gets paid to spend time with us, not to sit her ass in the supervisor's office. Do people even know she's there?"

"Go ahead and tell them," I said, kidding.

"Somebody should."

The next morning Deb sat at her desk, intently organizing her papers. "Michael," she said when she saw Rodney. "I didn't realize you were the vigilante of the textile world."

"We missed you, darlin'," Rodney said, leaning across the expanse of manila folders. "We needed a boss up here, a leader. We're lost without you. If I hadn't known better I would have thought you were avoiding me. And now, here you are."

"I'm here because I have something to say."

Someone, she told us, had mixed dye lots of Raisin while filling an order. As a result, a Scotch plaid had been woven incorrectly. Someone had also mixed dye lots of Fern for a special jacquard piece. This in particular had been an expensive, damaging mistake, but luckily for us, the supervisor was still in Rome, climbing renowned campaniles, studying paintings strewn with lush, fat-bottomed women splayed in tall grass. He was drinking carafes of house wine, lamenting the fact that he had not played golf in days. Most likely he wouldn't hear about this mistake, and if he did, he'd still be bloated and jet-lagged, apathetic to the fact that we'd even made it. Still, we couldn't have mistakes like these. If they continued, certain measures would have to be taken.

"You sound so serious," Rodney said and Deb stared out at us with the absent look of something carved. Her jawline suggested business. I considered the fact that she had never before taken things so seriously.

"Do you understand?"

"Certainly, darlin'," Rodney said. "Certainly, we understand."

On July Fourth we celebrated with a company picnic.

I'd never been a summer-holiday sort of person. I hated softball, had no interest in horseshoes, and worried about the integrity of the food, bacteria proliferating in the heat. We celebrated in the lethargic way of such holidays. Men drank beer with subdued melancholy while women huddled in groups, shifting their weight and pecking at macaroni salad, using their hands as ineffectual fans.

Rodney's wife, hearing that I worked with her husband, smiled and made polite conversation about why on earth had I decided to work here for the summer. I sipped my beer and told her this is what happened when you were forced to do things. She sipped her own beer and said, "I know the feeling."

I'd caught glimpses of her before this. She dropped Rodney off at work each morning and picked him up each afternoon, the boys wrestling the car's sticky summer leather into submission while they waited for him. She always gave Rodney a perfunctory kiss hello or goodbye, whatever was required of her, with the puckered look of someone who'd just sucked lemon. Her voice carried a high-voltage enthusiasm; the ends of words bristled like live wires. She was an attractive, overweight woman wearing so much rouge it gave her the farcical look of a scarecrow. She hovered above the apple crisp, making self-deprecating jokes about her utter lack of willpower and scooping the treat out of the container with an abandoned piece of cardboard; someone had forgotten serving utensils. She and Rodney spoke once that I saw, to discuss the proper level of punishment for their son's spitting in the supervisor's son's face. Leaning toward one another, discussing the inadequacies of various punishments, their energies repelled one another. The son stood sullen-faced and dirty, caught between the two of them like a gnat.

Rodney said, "I would have spit in his face, too." We had passed like ships in front of the chips and dip. Flies buzzed as he reached drunkenly for a chip. He said, "I would have punched him."

"He's nine."

"If I were nine, I would have punched him."

"He's a kid."

"He's an asshole of the future," Rodney said.

"You're the responsible one here," I said. "The adult."

He held a beer can nearly vertical above his mouth before saying, "Thanks for all the credit. Now, where's our little slut?"

He meant Deb, who came late, overdressed in a white dress that hung off her small frame like a bed sheet and stark, shiny jewelry that exposed the frailty of her neck and wrists. She looked less a slut than an angel in an elementary school play, minus the tinsel halo. They'd come late, Rodney pointed out, most likely to create an entrance in Deb's new car, a new SUV that gave her the look, when she was inside it, of having been swallowed by it. The car drove her, the way certain dogs walked their owners. She and Mitch had just come, literally, from the dealership. The paper detailing the car's price and various options was still taped to the window. Mitch leaned against the hood, telling the intricate details of how he'd successfully wrangled a bargain from the asshole salesperson. This was the first I'd heard Mitch speak. His words had the sound of someone gnawing hungrily on a bone. I strained to decipher them while he massaged the nape of Deb's neck with too much force. She swayed slightly with the motion, silently tilting her narrow cheekbones into the sun and looking as if she were imagining herself someplace entirely different, preferably a place where even an SUV couldn't go. I gave a wave hello in her direction, and she burrowed her cheekbones more deeply into the sun, as if we'd never uttered a single word to one another. It occurred to me, briefly, that since Rodney's arrival we'd barely spoken.

"What does he do?" I asked Rodney.

"Owns a lumberyard."

"Of course he does," I said. "Listen to the way he talks."

"Yeah, well."

"You know him?"

"We went to high school together. The three of us."

"You're friends?"

"He's an asshole," Rodney said, as if it were impossible for him to be lumped into this exact category. "He's always been an asshole." He stared at Mitch, currently examining a scratch on the SUV's passenger side door and expressing his garbled dismay over this.

"Looks like."

"Yeah, well."

We didn't speak again until much later, when the supervisor prepared to make company announcements. Rodney sidled beside me, hand circling my neck, and whispered with damp drunk breath into my ear, "Having fun yet?" His body, so closely beside me, emanated heat and masculinity, a vague contempt I could not quite place.

"Parties are work."

"Everything's work," he said. "Especially parties. Look at this guy," he said, waving toward the supervisor.

"I've known him since I was three," I said.

"That's not my problem."

The supervisor spoke with a muffled voice into the microphone, constantly smoothing his pleated pants, which gave him the look of a skirted sink. This particular July Fourth marked the longest stretch the company had ever gone without an accident. For six months, there had been no official record of a person severing or bludgeoning his own body part, stumbling into heavy machinery. *Congratulations!* The microphone groaned with distortion.

"Congratulations!" Rodney mimicked, drinking beer.

In commemoration, we were given coffee mugs emblazoned with AMERICAN SILK SAFETY AWARD in gold caps and filled to the brim with cheap dollar-store chocolate that Rodney, in his drunken haze, flicked into the grass, piece after dull piece, and which the children clamored for, fighting and lunging in the heat like sweaty, selfish demons.

"Fuck safety," Rodney said under his breath, but the words swelled, hung like orbs. "Like I fucking need chocolate. Like I fucking need any of this."

The holiday sputtered out with a sticky confluence of humidity and mishandled explosives. Even my mother, usually filled with heady optimism, was depressed. She had gone to the community fireworks display, where an incorrectly aimed roman candle shot into a truck where other fireworks were stored.

"I thought it was the *finale*," she said. "I sat there clapping, wanting more. I thought the entire thing was brilliant, the most spectacular show I'd ever seen, until the ambulance came. A man almost died."

"Nice, Mother," I said.

We returned to work on a Tuesday, and Deb told us: someone had mixed dye lots of Raisin for the second time. The weavers were now weaving this particular piece of fabric for the third time, thanks to my and Rodney's sheer ineptitude.

"Define *ineptitude*," Rodney said.

"Look it up," Deb said. "Or is that too difficult?"

We were, unfortunately, too hot to care about something as inconsequential as ineptitude, even our own. We took turns in the upstairs bathroom, washing our faces and armpits with soap that smelled like a convalescent home before wasting time on the fire escape, drinking stale paper cones of water and staring across the gravel glare of the parking lot. We said little, studying the parked cars, matching them to workers. The supervisor drove a new model Mustang meant to suggest his adventurous, youthful spirit, but which, truth be told, conveyed his undeniable ridiculousness. My own Volvo sat indestructible in its spot like a boulder. Deb's SUV loomed up like a growth in the asphalt, malignant. She had parked it slightly away from the mill workers' rows of beat-up Corollas and Civics, as if she didn't trust people and their need to slam doors.

"*Look* at that," Rodney said, staring across the refracted windshield light of the various cars, the glint and glare of chrome.

"Look at what?"

He tossed his empty paper cone over the edge of the fire escape and stalked silently inside.

Over the following week, as if to prove Deb's point, there were constant discrepancies, the subtlest shifts in shadings, in countless pieces of fabric. These discrepancies mainly involved the colors Fern, Chartreuse, and Persimmon. There were problems as well with Currant, with Cayenne and Canary. The ruined pieces of these fabrics were sent back to us, tacked with small notes penned by Milton, the angry man who inspected them, cursing his sour breath into their floral flourishes. His handwriting gave the impression of bees buzzing. Rodney and I stared at it, decoding. *Color shifts!!! Inaccurate dye lots!!! Not good!!!*

"He likes exclamation points," I observed. "That makes him unreliable."

Deb said, "You both need to be more astute."

"Astute?" Rodney asked. He loomed beside her, over her, touching his wide thumb to a green leaf situated prettily, so prettily, against

146

a background of cranberry. Neither he nor I could discern what the exact problem was, but it was there.

"Astute," Deb said. "*Astute.*" She held this word in her mouth, testing it as though for nuance, lingering over it like something possibly sweet.

"Whatever," Rodney interrupted. "Fucking whatever."

"Do you know how astute I am?" Rodney asked the next morning.

We had arrived late as usual, shocked into reality by the third floor's blatant humidity and the temperature, which Rodney registered by tapping his finger against the glass thermometer: one hundred degrees and climbing. Deb was already in the supervisor's office, discussing the problematic absence of one hundred pounds of Maple in the latest yarn shipment. Still, she'd managed to pin the ruined examples of yesterday's fabrics to the board beside her desk where we might consider them and be reminded our of dazzling ineptitude.

"Are you being rhetorical?"

"*This* is how astute I am," Rodney said. He picked up Deb's purse from the foot of her desk with dramatic flair, rifling inside it with even more dramatic flair before locating her wallet with its innumerable zippered pockets and slots for safekeeping. "Shit," he said, holding up a handful of cash. "I'll buy the drinks tonight. Are you free? Would you like to get a drink tonight?" Still holding the cash, he jangled her car keys. "I'll even drive."

"Are you *crazy?*"

"*Shhh,*" he said. Sliding both the cash and the keys into his front pocket, he disappeared downstairs.

He returned a while later, sweaty, slipping the keys back inside her purse as if they'd never been gone. In between thirsty sips of water he told me: he'd moved her car from the company parking lot—that protected, careful spot—three blocks away on the shoulder of a dubious, unpaved side street. He had also, just for good measure, removed all four of her hubcaps, flinging them individually, like Frisbees, into the tall grass. Her car, he noted approvingly, wasn't nice enough for mags, despite its expensive, happy glare.

"Nice, Rodney," I said. "You don't even have a car."

"I have a car," he said. "I don't have a license."

"Sorry," I said. "I forgot the distinction. What happened to your license?"

"Let's see if she's astute," Rodney said, ignoring me. "Let's see if she pays careful attention." Quoting her, his voice had a soothing quality, like a child's lullaby. "Let's see," he said, "if she has a problem getting a parking ticket. Or even a tow."

"You're an asshole," I said.

"I'm not," he said, "an asshole."

"You're daunted," I said, "by feminine authority."

"Haunted?"

"Daunted. And anyway," I said, "I'd like to point out that you're not even original. You're like some high school boy, heckling. You haven't progressed."

"Yeah, right," he said. But there was something in his voice that suggested this was, point of fact, his greatest fear. He had considered this, wondered over it.

"I've progressed," he said, and this was the lackluster defense he offered on his behalf.

The next morning, Deb gave no suggestion that anything was or had been amiss. She entered the third floor with the streamlined control of an airline stewardess, minus the outstretched-wing lapel pin and the accommodating demeanor. She'd pulled her hair back with a silk scarf, and this gave her an intimidating effect. Without missing a beat, she said, "Rodney, will you *please* organize the new shipment of Peach?"

He paused, guessing at what lay beneath the lines.

"*Rodney,*" she said.

Her acknowledgement of what had happened, though subtle, was evident as the day progressed and she kept her car keys in her purse and the purse on her person. When the supervisor phoned up, asking her to please meet him in his office, she slung the bag, leather and plump, over her shoulder rather than leave it behind.

She went downstairs, the purse banging heartily against her hip, or the straight line that should have been her hip, and I suspected she'd have a bruise there in the morning, blue and flourishing.

"Do you understand how much it will cost to weave this again?" Deb asked when she returned, unraveling fabric across her desk. Her face had sharpened like the tip of a pencil. Someone—really, Rodney or I—had mixed up dye lots of Apricot for an expensive piece of jacquard, and the supervisor had had quite a bit to say about this. "This fabric costs rich people a lot of money. Do you have any idea how much money?"

"Well, it's fucking ugly," Rodney said. "It's a lot of fuss over something ugly."

The three of us stood for a moment, staring at it. The fabric *was* ugly, suggestive of a room in which no one had anything to say to one another and absolutely nothing to do. It was the sort of distracting fabric, with its ornate flourishes, that would have a proximity to precious-metal knickknacks and candelabra. Its gold furls reminded us: we did not have the power to special order something so ugly simply because we wanted it. By default we were destined to plain, mass-produced fabrics, plaids and ginghams, things that came in plastic packaging.

"It's pretty ugly," I said while Deb refolded the jacquard meticulously, corner to corner, smoothing as she folded, her face pinched in concentration.

"I didn't ask for your opinion," she said. "I don't care about your opinion."

"You care about it," Rodney said.

"No," she said. "I really don't."

"You're lazy," Deb reminded us constantly, with clearly articulated consonants. She acted as if she and I had never had a conversation; she'd never given up secrets over too many fuzzy navels; she'd never let down her guard. We had never been friends, even of the thrown-together variety. What she said to me fell into the category of requests: *Please move the box of Violet out of the aisle. Please fill these orders first. Please stop being so lazy.* Her voice had an unrelenting, almost formal, politeness. When I asked her, one *lazy* afternoon, if she wanted to go to the bar that night for a drink, she clamped her shoulder blades together so fiercely I waited to hear the clang of them. She said, with the trace of what I perceived to be irony, "Ask Rodney," and I felt accused of something indiscernible.

It was August. Rodney and I struggled in the heat. The cones of yarn—two pounds, four pounds at most—felt terrifically heavy, like dumbbells we hadn't yet mastered the art of lifting. We took a great many breaks—water breaks and snack breaks, radio breaks. It took extraordinary energy to lift soda cans to our mouths, to shell sunflower seeds, to drink water.

And then, one morning near the end of the month, we realized someone had stuck the wrong cones inside every box. Black Sabbath played menacingly from the radio. The air throbbed. Dust crowded around us.

"No fucking way!" Rodney said. We opened more boxes, testing them. A cone of Plum had been stuck inside Violet. Juniper had been put inside Cayenne. Canary was inside Dust, Olive inside Persimmon, Aubergine inside Black. Inside a box of Lemon I found Watermelon, Rust, and Clove. Rodney, scrambling for fifteen pounds of Ocean for an important order, discovered instead the mere remnants of several skeins that he sent scuttling across the floor.

"What the fuck!" Rodney said, punching a box of Papaya. "What the fuck! It's sabotage!"

"All right, crazy," I said. "All right, Stevie."

"I'm not Stevie. Don't even call me that."

"Maybe it was an accident."

"Like this was an accident."

Over lunch, he'd calmed down sufficiently to recount the stories he'd read, snippets in the newspapers over time: a waitress who'd placed a roach into the salad mixture; a man who released a frog into the machine that mashed the blueberries for a well-known brand of frozen pie; a fast-food worker who'd dipped customers' shrimp into the filmy mop water before frying. And, of course, there were examples involving guns and public-service workers, post officers and policemen who simply, completely, lost it. Neurons misfired, synapses broke, and the result was carnage: sobbing family members, bloodied linoleum, ruined lives.

"It's her," he said. "*Deb.*"

"She wants to blow our heads off?"

"She's doing this to me."

"That's egotistical."

"Yeah, well. I'm an egotistical prick."

"Finally," I said. "Self-reflexivity!"

"I have no idea what the fuck you're talking about," Rodney said. "I have no idea what that means." He gnawed at the crust on his sandwich as if had done something offensive to him and he was putting it in its place. "Her husband thinks she's a model citizen. He's too stupid to get it. You've seen him. He's a giant walking and talking block."

"What you're saying is crazy," I said.

"Did I fucking ask for your opinion?"

He did not say another word to me until we were leaving. Standing on the slab of concrete between the building and the parking lot, he lit a cigarette and gave a nod in my direction. "What do you care about any of this? You're leaving."

"I'm leaving, sure."

"You have no reason to care about anything that happens here."

"Sure I do."

"No, you don't."

He dropped his smoke onto the cement, giving it a single scuff with his heel before setting out across the gravel lot. He went with lengthy strides, kicking at the occasional lone yarn cone or slivery bit of leftover gum wrapper, and as he did, I shouted after him, "What about your *ride?*"

Turning, framed by a backdrop of afternoon sun, he resembled a disgraced hero from a comic book. Standing like this, dark and mysterious against the glare, he gave me the finger.

\* \* \*

His wife, it turned out, was away. She'd taken the car. He told me two days later, on a Wednesday, as if it had taken him forty-eight hours to acknowledge the fact that she was actually gone. She was in Allentown with the kids, visiting her mother, who had an aboveground swimming pool and satellite television, a junk-food drawer, an RV for wilderness excursions.

"It's a regular palace of vacation," he said, irony flaring inside his voice.

"Doesn't school start soon?" I asked. "Like, next week?"

He shrugged. "Maybe they'll be back, maybe not."

"She should have left you the car."

"What good is a fucking car," he asked, "without a license?"

"Fine," I said. "Valid point."

"Of course it's a goddamn valid point."

"Of course," I said.

He smelled of beer. Emanated it.

"You've been drinking."

"So?"

"You're at *work*. You could get *fired*."

"Please, dear God!"

"Nice, Rodney."

He said, "We're getting a drink tonight."

"We are?"

"It's my gift to you, before you go."

"Great."

"Don't sound too excited," he said, words slurry, before pushing himself away from me and toward the radio, bending over the dial with an elaborate concentration.

That afternoon, he swaggered, drunk, toward Deb's desk and demanded without a preamble of any sort, "What are you doing here late at night when you should be cooking dear, darling Mitchell his dinner? Mike from weaving says you can't get enough of this place. He says you're here by yourself, passing time, doing *Lord knows what*, fucking up *God knows what* for the rest of us, when you should be spending time with your husband."

"Mike who?"

"Mike from weaving."

"I have no idea," she said, "what you're talking about. I don't know Mike from weaving."

"You know him."

"I don't." She paused, and in that pause she located her weaponry from wherever she'd misplaced it. She asked, "And anyway, what's your wife doing in Allentown?"

"A vacation."

"I see," Deb said. "An indefinite one, if she has any sense."

"You always were so funny," Rodney said. "So fucking funny. It's what I remember most about you."

"I doubt that," Deb said. "I doubt that's what you remember."

That night, my mother eyed me curiously before I left to meet Rodney. "You're too young," she said, "to like wounded older men. You have a father—you shouldn't have these sorts of issues. Also, you're too young to go to a bar as often as you do. Save that for when you're forty and desperate."

"He isn't that old," I said. "I don't like him. It isn't like that."

"There's a desperation you know nothing about."

"Fine," I said. "All right."

"I'm right," my mother said. "I'm always right."

Because Rodney couldn't drive, I picked him up. The house, which he rented, was a bi-level with half-dead bushes careening to one side as if there'd been a recent, unrelenting storm. The windows were shrouded in sterile white mini-blinds that the cat, jumping onto the windowsill, had bent with his constant craning head. I waited in the living room, sitting on a couch that had a child's bed sheet thrown over it, alternating my attention between the rocket ships printed on the bed sheet and the carpet, a discomfiting pea-green color. The requisite JC Penney or Sears photos of the children lined the wall, the boys sitting on carpet-covered boxes and clutching limp stuffed animals. They stared unblinkingly at the camera in their tiny flannels and overalls. Implied beyond their line of vision was the photographer, most likely a person ringing a bell or shaking a rubber chicken, urging smiles. There was the scent in the room of something odd, slight but prevalent—distant cat piss or mildew, mold.

"All right," Rodney said. He appeared in the doorway, dressed for the occasion in a button-down shirt whose chaotic flourishes would have favored no one, but certainly did not favor *him,* a man destined for plain, solid colors and efficient, skin-conforming cuts, something Marlon Brando might have worn in his better days. Rodney's voice already had a drunken, self-conscious slur, as if he'd already contemplated the ridiculousness of his outfit and yearned to be the man who could pull off the grand patterns and ornate belt buckles and snakeskin boots. He adjusted himself in his shirt, slightly too big, and his hand made its way to the crook of my hip. I had the feeling his hand didn't quite want to be there, but since it was, it needed to be chivalrous, committed to the fact that it was. His body vibrated the subtle tension of this dilemma. He asked, "Are we ready?"

I guessed that we were.

We went to the same bar I'd gone to with Deb, with its accumulation of softball trophies and moth-eaten pennants pinned to the walls, its teetering karaoke stage. A man stood nervously when we entered, preparing to sing "Total Eclipse of the Heart." Rodney slid despondently onto a barstool. "Why do I come here?"

"Because you like it?"

He scoffed loudly into his drink.

"Okay," I said. "You don't like it."

He frowned deeply while I feigned interest in the karaoke singers. The women, especially, attacked notes as if the notes had made threats on their lives. They wrangled notes, threw them onto the metaphoric ground, stomped them down. The bar air had a dusty quality. Strung lights shimmered and blinked.

Rodney said, "Sheila took the kids to Allentown."

"You told me."

"I mean, she *took* the kids to Allentown."

"Is she leaving you?"

"Sounds like," he said.

"For good?"

"Could be." He sucked noisily from his glass. "Hard to tell. Check back, and I'll let you know. Oh, wait, you're leaving. You won't be back. You won't be checking."

"Do you love her?"

"Sure, why not?"

"That's ambiguous."

"It is what it is."

"How philosophical."

"I'm a philosophical genius."

I took this awkward moment to order another fuzzy navel. A woman with too much foundation cracked onto her face stood to sing Whitney Houston. Her voice had a strange warble on the high notes, like vomit had just climbed up her throat and she was fighting it back down. The waitress set my drink down with a clatter.

"Well, all right, Deborah," Rodney said. He, too, motioned for another.

"How do you know her drink?"

"*Everyone* knows her drink." He gave a lithe, inebriated shrug. "She's that kind of woman."

"A one-drink woman," I said.

"It's the only thing she's singular about," he said. "Trust me."

"Why did you tell her all that stuff about Mike from jacquards? Is there even a Mike from jacquards?"

He peered into his glass.

"No," I answered. "There isn't."

"Mitch believes there is."

"Rodney, you're sick."

"I'm a sick puppy," he agreed.

"Why do you hate her?"

"I don't."

"Right," I said.

"I *love* her. I've always loved her." He spoke as if quoting a song, something from the karaoke listing. "I'm surprised, smart college girl, that you can't figure out such an obvious fucking thing. I'm disappointed."

"Are you kidding me?"

"What, am I being too *maudlin* for you, Emma? I wouldn't want to be too *maudlin*."

"Rodney," I said and he refused to answer me. "*Rodney*," I said, and he ignored me, focusing his attention inside the world of his glass, the manageable, distinct world of ice and bourbon. He tilted it slightly to the right and then to the left, as if to gain a keener perspective.

"Rodney."

"Shut up," he said.

The next morning I went to work, hungover and apprehensive about seeing him: I'd left him there, midsong, weaving on his barstool, trying to keep his balance on it. I left and didn't care how he got home, what happened to him. I needn't have worried. He came the next morning with the lingering scent of whiskey, seemingly ignorant to the fact that I'd even abandoned him. He came to work drunk, hiding beer cans on the second-tier shelving so they wouldn't be easily noticed and drinking from several different cans scattered throughout the aisles. He passed the morning staggering into boxes, dropping his X-Acto knife, picking it up, dropping it.

Deb avoided this situation entirely, intently gathering papers up from her desk and not glancing in Rodney's direction.

She had, I couldn't help noticing in the moments before she finally went downstairs, a bruise below her left collarbone. She'd done nothing specifically to cover it, as if she wanted people—someone, really—to see it. It was simply *there,* staining the expanse of her skin. It looked at once damning and beautiful, floral, as if opening itself to the sun. Had it not been a bruise it might have been almost decorative, a pin, a brooch, something attached to a lapel, something people might bend toward and say, Well look at that.

"Right," she said with flippant irony when she noticed my stare. "I hurt myself. Stupid." She clanked her thin shoulders together in a shrug.

"Rodney," I said, accosting him in the aisle that housed the M's and N's and P's, colors like Midnight and Nero and Pumpkin.

"It was Mitch," he said. "It wasn't me."

"Right. *You* would have never done such a thing. You're too upstanding."

"Fuck off," he said.

"You're pathetic," I said, "crazy," and as if to prove his clear delusional tendencies, or as if he wanted one last-ditch effort to provide an argument for himself, he wrenched my wrist, pulled me close, and kissed me. It was a kiss that held a great deal of pressure, a possibly combustible kiss, as if he'd dropped something inside my mouth and was searching furiously for it. His kissing gave my mouth the sensation of being scraped raw, though there was no logical reason to think this.

"Forget it," Rodney said, pulling away, wiping his mouth with his hand.

"What?" I asked and tried to sound polite.

"Your charity."

"There's no charity," I lied.

He said, "You've never been forced to do anything in your entire life."

"Maybe," I said.

"I know it. Like the back of my hand."

"Yeah, well," I said. An uncomfortable moment passed between us, and in an uncanny instant, we both craned our heads to the clock, barely visible from where we stood. We were unified, briefly, in the understanding that this exchange had taken only seconds; we'd accomplished nothing, neither of us, in that passage of time.

# CARE

This year, her thirtieth year, her body has given her breasts. Much like the first wedding anniversary is the paper one and the eleventh is the anniversary of steel, her thirtieth birthday is the birthday of sudden, unexpected femininity. In the bar, sitting beside Hayes, Theresa cups one full breast in each hand and they are, in this cupping, heavy enough to be paperweights, heavy enough to provide a reliable buoyancy should she be thrown, flailing, into the ocean. She sips carefully at her bourbon and tells Hayes: she has always considered her breasts something like a mysterious relative. They choose their infrequent appearances with care. The last she feels she really saw of them, she was ten years old and in the fourth grade. She'd honed a frumpy unpopularity without the added liability of precocious breasts. She wore sweatpants and ugly floral shirts more suitable for forty-year-olds. She wore bobos. She had an inexplicable obsession with astronauts and outer space.

"I remember," Hayes says, "the girls with bobos. Bobos were, like, the grade-school equivalent of the plague."

"Thank you," Theresa says. "It's all coming back to me."

They are sitting in their usual seats at the farthest corner of the bar. Hayes is drinking something pink from a stem glass. Theresa is drinking bourbon over ice, a celebratory birthday drink, courtesy of Hayes. At this particular moment, the ice in the glass looks determined to slice her throat on its way down. Normally she lets the ice melt into the bourbon slowly, suggestively, the way ice does, but tonight this demands a more refined patience than she feels capable of. Because she drinks bourbon, Hayes likes to say that she is the man in their relationship—he, of course, is the woman—but now, with the arrival of her latent breasts, her role is suddenly confused. At age thirty she will no longer be able to run for miles without wearing a bra. Regardless of the fact that she never runs—she would run, maybe, *possibly*, if someone were chasing her—this small fact depresses her. These breasts, this heaviness, signals the beginning of the end: adulthood, disappointment.

"I would have baked a cake," Hayes says, "but you know I don't bake. You know I falter in the face of precision."

"I do," she says. They toast a weary toast.

They are at a gay bar, having flipped a quarter to decide: gay or straight? Each of them would like a man to take home, but they can't both in this particular situation, unless Theresa is fortunate enough to happen upon a nice bisexual man, something she's realizing never happens. Right now Hayes is evaluating the men who pass by with an efficient yet subtle once-over. He holds the stem of his glass between two fingers and tells her: last night he slept with the Channel 6 sportscaster.

"You did not!" Theresa says.

"I did."

Hayes thinks this sportscaster is a precious mineral of a man, like a piece of tiger's eye, but Theresa knows that Hayes is not actually discriminating in his selection of lovers. He sleeps with anyone, people she wouldn't share a bus seat with. She watches this particular sportscaster for her Steelers coverage and has always considered him borderline cross-eyed. His forehead has always seemed too large, stretched across his face like a piece of canvas. Now, in retrospect, his football lingo seems too obviously ironic: *good penetration in the backfield, going deep, third and long.* She never would have guessed he was gay. She would have thought, instead, he'd beaten up more than a few gay men, bruised their skin, roughened their delicate egos.

"He had beer cans all over the floor, the counter, everywhere," Hayes tells her. "There wasn't room to walk. The sportscaster is a drunk, an absolute and complete drunk. And also," Hayes says. "He couldn't perform. As a result, this was an angry experience, as far as experiences go—nearing abusive, like he wanted to punish me. If I had been in a different mood, maybe, I could have enjoyed it."

"Please," Theresa says, forcing this word out from inside a sudden swell of her own drunkenness. It feels like this takes a great deal of energy to do, like extricating a particularly embedded rock from dry soil.

"Incidentally," Hayes says. "While we're on this subject of sex. I have something that looks like an actual lesion, like you always hear about."

"In the circles I hang with," she says, "lesions aren't actually conversation pieces."

"You hang with me," Hayes says. "And I am, actually, talking about lesions."

"Please don't," she says, but he is already pushing up his shirtsleeve to show her. On the pale underside of his arm is something that could in fact be a lesion. Theresa doesn't know. She's never seen one before, though she's read about them—in the Bible, in the passages about lepers. Jesus touched the lepers, he smoothed their lesions with the healing power of his tanned hands, and he cured them. Hayes touches his own possible lesion gingerly, as if to cause it to jump up and walk away. He has told her this, he is showing her this, because they are drunk and in this condition, willing to overshare. They are willing to stand, shaky, on the thin limbs of their emotions.

"Lesions," he says, "are a symptom of nothing good. I went to the doctor," he says. "I got tested for HIV."

"You don't have HIV," she says.

"Like you know."

"Go to University Health. They'll call it mono, no matter what the symptoms. Mono is their preferred diagnosis. It doesn't intimidate them like other diagnoses."

"I'm not going to University Health," Hayes says. He drinks the last of his drink, motions to the bartender for another.

She shrugs. "Anyway, about my breasts."

"That," he says. "I'll grant you a few pounds apiece. I noticed it, and I never notice breasts unless they're, like, a Halloween gag and on a man."

"These," she says, "are real."

"They certainly are."

"Touch them and see."

"No, thank you," Hayes says. "No touching."

The bourbon has made her weepy. She is on the pesky edge of crying. She feels like she is standing on the sliver of a precipice, staring down at something unidentifiable. Even the people around her are depressing, drinking well liquor and struggling to have conversation. They're all wanting love, and failing. They're settling, instead, for cocktails made with real fruit juice.

"We're good friends," she tells Hayes, "but we aren't tender. Sometimes I need to feel tender, like I've been pounded down and salted."

"As we get older," Hayes says, "these are the sorts of desperate conversations we want to avoid."

"I'm not desperate."

"I'm just saying," Hayes says. "You have the potential."

They share a cubicle. Together, they are a blight of their department. They have reputations for killing potentially interesting conversations in one fell swoop, as if taking a hatchet to them. They are first-year teaching assistants in English literature, teaching the freshman composition course Concepts of Care: Family, Community, Society. In this course they are meant to use the topic of caring—the myriad ways that people care for others—as a vehicle to educate their students about reading and writing.

"I don't care," her students say in response to her questions. "Who cares?" they ask, and think this is a wonderful joke. Their students are what the professors of the teaching seminars would call *resistant readers*; they are resistant to thinking about the discourse of care, much like Hayes and Theresa are resistant to teaching it. Hayes, always out on a limb with his pedagogy, doesn't bother with the primary text. He shows movies. *One Flew Over the Cuckoo's Nest* took up an entire week's classes.

"They didn't get it," he says.

"What are they supposed to be getting?" Theresa asks. She quotes something she read in the teaching seminar packet before the semester had even started: "These readings are not something your students can get, like bread at the store."

"I wanted to show," Hayes says, "the sometimes negative effects of public caregiving."

"Oh, that," Theresa says.

"I myself," Hayes says, "am impervious to care. I'm impervious to caregiving *and* receiving."

It is the morning after Theresa's birthday. Tomorrow is the start of Thanksgiving break. There is one final paper to grade before the semester portfolios, and then they are free, free. Because tomorrow is the start of break, Theresa and Hayes have both canceled their classes for today; they have not even bothered going to campus. They have come, instead, to Theresa's favorite café, where she spends hours each day, spreading her belongings across several tables at once, as if this café is her living room. Here, she pretends she is a social being. In between her own readings—*Renaissance Discourses of Gender*, for instance, or *The Nationalist Resolution of the Women's Question*—she amuses herself by staring at the baristas, attractive though possibly—most likely—too thin and young and hip for her. She has imagined straddling their young bodies only to crush their delicate bones with the magnitude of her thighs; has imagined them shattering beneath her like fragile chickens.

Theresa taps at the student paper before her. "Listen to this: *This author is a lesbian. As readers, she does not give respite to the plain fact that she hates men. This thought occurs many times throughout the chapter and she does not want us to forget it, the plain fact that men are pigs.*"

"I'm happy," Hayes says, "to be leaving."

"It's not actually a vacation."

"If there's a hotel, it's a vacation. I adore hotels."

"They've done tests on hotel bedspreads and found," Theresa says, "like, six hundred samples of semen on a single comforter."

"I like semen," Hayes says. "I will not allow you to ruin my fun."

They plan to visit her father in New Jersey. This is not what could be called a typical visit; he doesn't even know she's coming. This fact—that he does not know she is coming—is a built-in safety mechanism, like the latches on trunks that permit you to exit should you happen to get trapped inside. She has not spoken to her father, she has not seen him, since she was eight years old. She would not have considered speaking to him if she had not gotten a rambling message on her answering machine nearly two months ago. It was a woman's voice, pausing, starting, stopping: "Our grandfather is dying. He's on his deathbed and asking for you. I've called Theresa Roberts everywhere, in every state. If this is you, please, call me." Theresa felt bad that she was not the person this woman was looking for. She meant to call her and tell her she'd gotten another wrong number—*sorry,* good luck. She told this story to her mother, trying to make a joke out of it, but her mother pointed out that she was, actually, the person this woman was looking for. The cousin's name is Caroline, and Theresa has pictures of the two of them as six-year-olds celebrating Easter, clutching cellophane-wrapped chocolate bunnies in their laps, their Easter dresses spread pink and stiff and proper around them. She has pictures of the two of them posing for the camera on one birthday or another, a rumpled pin-the-tail-on-the-donkey poster tacked to the wall as backdrop.

"That man," her mother said, and Theresa drew a mental picture of the grandfather in question, ill and intimidating, the scent of something she now understands was rot coming from his mouth. He made a habit of walking around the house dressed in sagging, sallow underwear. Her father she remembers as tall and imposing, bearded. When she was so young, bearded men seemed to her generally creepy. She lumped them in the same category of men who drove suspicious vans and lured young children with bits of candy, who wore stained jeans that never fit right.

"He's still alive?" her mother wanted to know. She approached the topic in the removed manner in which she might discuss the ridiculous plot twists of her least favorite soap opera. "*Back then* he was on the brink of death. And he wants to see you? He's seen you maybe ten times total. *Asking for you on his deathbed.*"

"He could have," Theresa said. Her ego felt slightly bruised, like she should not bother leaning on it for support. "Who's to say I'm not deathbed material?"

"Go if you want," her mother said.

"We could talk," Theresa said. "You and I. We could have an actual conversation."

"About what?"

"If it isn't completely obvious to you," Theresa said, "never mind."

Hayes, drawn to histrionic drama as he was, loved the potential of this narrative and its nearly stock soap-operatic characters: the confused daughter, the absent father, and silent mother. When he made the suggestion that they visit over Thanksgiving break, Theresa guessed he'd scraped at an idea that had always been there, simmering. She agreed to it because the entire situation had seemed to her inevitable, something she'd been moving toward, even imagining, for years, though not with the luster she once had. She got the necessary information from Caroline, the cousin who left the message, though Theresa refused telling her the specifics of when she was coming, and for how long. Her cousin had an exasperated quality to her voice, like someone had tightened it with a wrench. This voice told Theresa a great deal about her. She was the type of woman who cooked with Tuna Helper, who found comfort in the afternoon television programming, and who insulted her own children when she was angry. She wanted better things for herself, had imagined life differently. Theresa promised to call her when and if she arrived and had the awkward moment of realizing, as she said it, that her promises were frequently noncommittal.

Hayes, with his love of forced theatrics, had taken it upon himself to schedule a tune-up at her father's garage the day before Thanksgiving. "It's a holiday," Hayes told her. "A very busy time. And still, I managed it—I insisted on an appointment. You'll be seeing him as a client now, not a daughter. You'll have level footing. You can refuse to pay if you don't like the service. You can call the Better Business Bureau. It's, like, a form of recon."

"Recon," Theresa said, tiredly.

"*Reconnaissance,*" Hayes clarified with a flair he seemed to think was French.

"I know what it means."

"You can decide to attack, or you can decide to retreat."

"You're very weird," Theresa said.

"It's ridiculous," Hayes agreed.

"And on your thirtieth birthday!" he says now, around a mouthful of croissant. "We need to make it before the grandfather dies."

"He'll hold out," Theresa says. "Supposedly he's resilient. Supposedly he looks dead but lives forever."

"Here's hoping," Hayes says.

They sip at their coffees, and Theresa reads aloud from the paper before her, "*Language is the backbone of everything which is here and not here. It tells us what is what and what is not what. The epigraph quote,* constant shifting of the phantasmagoria, *is telling us that things are constantly shifting. Without this line to describe things, everything would be abstract. I apply this to* A Very Easy Death *in the way that Simone's life is constantly shifting.*"

"Be delicate," Hayes says.

"I am," Theresa says. "I will."

"I mean, be delicate to *me*," Hayes says. "I mean, be delicate to my life."


"Ah, the City of Brotherly Love," Hayes says that afternoon when Theresa pulls the car through the turnpike booth.

"I don't think it's called that anymore," Theresa says.

"How ominous."

Theresa has heard that traveling with someone is a true test of friendship, just as living together is the true test of a relationship, the ultimate comprehensive exam on the topic of love. Entire friendships, she understands, have unraveled midcountry, in the flat heat of places like Kansas and Missouri, when fatigue and depression set in, when too many Christian radio stations crowd the dials. Entire relationships have ended amid Ikea bookshelves and bargain wineglasses.

She and James had not lived together. They'd started out in neighboring dorms and had, each subsequent year, moved farther away from one another. By the seventh year, she drove on the freeway to see him, through the Squirrel Hill tunnel, past several exits, past Three Rivers Stadium and over a bridge to the North Side, then walked up a flight of stairs, through several rooms. Now he lives in Philadelphia—the city not of brotherly love, but of something— separated from her by an entire length of a state, with different neighboring states, different borders. He lives in a household of men-who-would-be-boys, who play instruments and drink too much, who lack careers and prefer spontaneous jobs they can ditch on a moment's notice. They wait tables and move rich people's furniture. He is—she's heard—seeing a woman he doesn't love but who is easy to manage, like uncomplicated finances. He seems happy, each time she talks to him, to not have to care specifically for someone. At one time he had cared for her with a precise ferocity not unlike caring for a wound, though this was something he had gotten over years before it had actually ended.

Already she knows already that she will call James; she will lure him into meeting her. They could have drunken inconsequential conversation, even more drunken and inconsequential sex that she could subside on for weeks as if these acts were a complex grain, something not easily digested.

On her own, she prefers to drive straight through; she prefers to stop for nothing. Hayes, however, is one of those people who want to stop at all the rest stops, no matter if they are actually hungry or thirsty or in need of rest. She forces herself to stand patiently beside him at the souvenir stand of one rest stop or other while he examines everything: the floating-scene ballpoint pens, the pencils capped with bright feathers, the teddy bears wearing *Pennsylvania* t-shirts. He turns several bears upside-down as if studying the quality of their fur. He puts them back, spins the postcards in their revolving display. Hayes has a thing for postcards. This is, he's told her, how he told his parents he was gay, with a postcard sent through the mail, addressed and stamped and postmarked.

"Did they write back?" Theresa had asked, joking.

"I sent the postcard at the beginning of fall semester my junior year, and we didn't speak until Christmas. When we did, finally, it was all very ambiguous, nothing about being gay, just, *All right, of course, as long as you're careful. As long as you're safe. You are being safe?* What's safe? Hayes asks. "What is that?"

"Safe," Theresa said. "You know, *safe.*"

"Right," Hayes said. "That."

They eat lunch in a fast-food pizzeria that also serves spaghetti with various sauces scooped up from the depths of silver serving trays. Everything about the food has a faux quality to it: faux cheese, faux tomato, faux garlic.

"It will be better," Hayes says, "at the hotel."

Their hotel is more than they can afford; their teaching stipends do not encourage the use of hotels. They have booked an especially nice room in Philadelphia despite their actual lack of money, because, as Hayes pointed out, it's Thanksgiving, and they should surround themselves with things they'd like to give thanks for. Without the possibility of being thankful for beautiful things, Hayes has said, they will each fall into deep ruts, exorbitant depressions that neither of them can afford. They are both susceptible to such depressions. In the thick of one, she disconnects the telephone, draws the blinds. She cries rivers. Hayes eats: packages of Jimmy Dean sausage biscuits, gallons of ice cream, entire cakes. He used to be seventy pounds heavier, he's told her, though she doesn't believe this. He mentions it again, his positive corpulence, as they finish the last of their pasta.

"Maybe I'll get fat again," Hayes says, stabbing a cube of mozzarella with his fork. "Gain another fifty or sixty pounds. It simplifies things."

"You were never fat," Theresa says.

"I was fat. It's what I did as a teenager. I ate. I had this girlfriend—she was a nice, unattractive fat girl, and I dreaded her. We didn't have sex; we ate. I ate and ate as if it would put literal, physical distance between us. Eating was the only thing I liked. The entire situation was embarrassing. Remind me," he says, "to tell you my most embarrassing story ever. It involves Oprah."

"Oprah *Winfrey*?" she asks.

Their three days at this hotel cost an entire month's stipend, two months' rent. Theresa will put the full amount on her credit card. The extravagance of something like a luxury hotel room is unfamiliar to her. This, however, is how Hayes was raised. He has spent time in hotels. He has spent time at his parents' billowy white country club and passed summers in Palm Springs, in his parents' second home, decorated in washed out pinks and peaches, with watercolors of sailboats on the walls and fat-lipped fish sculptures crowding the coffee tables. He had, as a teenager, his own credit card to do with as he pleased.

At the hotel, Hayes checks in. He rests his weight on a single strong elbow and leans toward the desk clerk.

"And your swimming pool?" Hayes asks. He turns to Theresa, pleased to discover: the swimming pool is on the roof, heated and ready for use despite the fact that it is almost winter.

"Fabulous!" he says. Theresa could care less about this amenity, but Hayes wants to sit by the pool with a cocktail. He wants to pretend that he is on a cruise ship, or the beach. Theresa typically admires Hayes's unnatural enthusiasm for unobvious pleasures, but right now she can't summon the energy. She feels tired and potentially weepy, like she is the crust at the corner of someone's eye, and it's the eye of a person she doesn't even like. She wants to curl into bed and watch mind-damaging television. She wants to order room service without having to pay for it. She wants bourbon. She wants sleep. She wants, she wants.

At the hotel bar, Hayes, always pleased by the prospect of colorful garnishes looming over his drink—poorly crafted Asian umbrellas, cheerful bits of fruit—orders a mai tai. The bartender smiles at him over the pouring and the stirring, the adding of a maraschino cherry.

"Is this really appropriate?" the bartender wants to know, nodding at the drink. He is—has to be—gay, with defiant-seeming bone structure and blond hair that appears to have been intentionally chlorine-damaged.

"Actually," Hayes says. "Make it two. I don't want to get up for a second drink. I shouldn't have to exert myself on vacation."

"Fine," the bartender says. "Of course." He stands smiling, the stem of a maraschino cherry slack in his hand. Something has passed between them in this moment. Theresa has felt it, like a short but exhilarating shock. "Where are you visiting from?" the bartender wants to know.

"Pittsburgh."

"Pittsburgh," the bartender repeats as though Pittsburgh is remarkably foreign, its own humble Sri Lanka or Kazakhstan.

"I'd like bourbon," Theresa interrupts. "Neat."

"Thanks for that," Hayes tells her when they have collected their drinks and passed safely out of the bartender's earshot. He holds a mai tai in each hand, each festooned with an umbrella.

"You're HIV positive," Theresa says. "You don't need a bartender." She thought that he would laugh, or at least smile, but Hayes stalks inside the elevator without a word.

"I'm sorry," Theresa says. "I thought you would laugh."

"I'm emphatically *not* laughing," he says. He sucks vigorously at his straw.

"Okay," she says. "All right."

The pool area is barren when they reach it, though the patio furniture is arranged as if it is still the height of summer, each sleek chair set appropriately in its place. The furniture appears agitated, as if it's had too much caffeine and is forcing itself to behave. The pool holds what appears to be dark, dangerous water. Hayes drags two lounge chairs to its edge, and they sit in cumbersome silence.

"I might call James," Theresa says. She is trying to make small talk, to undo her faux pas.

"Don't."

"I might," she says.

"The past," Hayes says, "is an ugly business. It's like a mean, dispirited virus. It'll suck you in and spit you out disoriented and disfigured."

"That," Theresa says, "was even more histrionic than the discourse of care."

"Whatever," Hayes says. "It's true." He has stood up. In the dim lighting, the corners of him angled in shadow, he begins stripping off his layers of clothes. He shucks them off like husks: first his woolen jacket, next his nicely pressed oxford. He folds everything neatly, corner to corner, cuff to cuff, and organizes it at the end of a lounge chair.

"What are you doing?"

"Obviously, I want to swim."

"Your imminent nakedness," Theresa says, "is unnerving." She tries not to look as Hayes slips off his jeans. He stands for a moment wearing only his boxers, wonderfully orange, and shivering in the cold. And then, quickly, he slips off the boxers. Standing naked like this, he appears translucent, like delicate china, and Theresa is impressed with his muscles, all making their sudden cameos as he bends, one last time, to organize the pile of clothes on the lounge chair. The men she dates are never athletic. They are artsy, musical, afraid of the sun, and soft like custard, like something to dip a spoon into. James, for sport, occasionally did not mind a good game of ping-pong, which he'd played with an uncanny aggression. She herself had never passed the fitness assessment in school. She never ran the mile in under ten minutes; she never did a pull-up; she never touched her toes. She failed gym class one semester in high school, and her mother had asked, "Who actually *fails* gym class?" Theresa had had to say, then: *she* was the sort who failed gym class, the same person who failed driver's ed and one semester of shop—of course she did not know how to construct her own bookcase. In high school, her mother ran track. She ran cross-country. Somewhere, though her mother does not remember where, are the medals to prove that she has won things. She has been the best, and for various indiscernible reasons, she likes Theresa to remember this.

"You won't do it! You won't go in!" Theresa calls across the pool the moment before Hayes dives, and he hits the water cleanly. He swims with a neat ferocity she's never seen translated into his daily actions, the teaching of classes, the grading of papers, the analysis of text, the contribution of mundane small talk. *Of course the language undermines the feminist agenda.* Something in the exacting movements of his arms and legs is intensely personal, suggests that he is working out something complicated in the process of his strokes. Watching Hayes swim, Theresa has the feeling of infringing. She's eavesdropping without listening, and hearing things despite this. For a moment, sitting on the proper and polite lounge chair that genuinely seems to care about the comfort of her back, she feels moody and alone.

In the room, she dials James's number from the softness of the hotel bed. The phone rings and rings; it rings and rings. She's about to hang up—it would be better, really, to just hang up—when a woman answers with a specific breathiness that tells Theresa she is not the easily managed and unloved girlfriend. This woman is someone completely different.

"Who's this?" Theresa demands of the receiver and understands: she has reached that point in her life where she won't even try to stop herself from doing embarrassing things; she has lost all sense of pride. This should bother her but she finds herself relinquishing herself to it, like someone caught in a violent current.

"Who's *this*?" the voice on the other end of the line asks, velvety and confident, and she is asking it again in the moment that Theresa finally does hang up. "Who's *this*?"

In the morning they order room service, imperfect and expensive. The foam in their cappuccinos is flat. Hayes has requested an over-abundance of pastry: scones and muffins, almond croissants and chocolate croissants. Hayes and Theresa wrap themselves in their complimentary bathrobes and pick halfheartedly at morning buns. Theresa cannot help thinking that this complimentary bathrobe feels softer than her own skin; this hotel uses better quality soap for its bathrobes than she uses on her own face. She settles more deeply into the robe, works through the channels on the television. Channel 41 is playing a Christian program, its evangelist especially mesmerizing in a sparkly maroon shirt. His mouth opens with surprising elasticity, as if God is working him from the inside, like a sock puppet.

"According to the scary man on television," Theresa says, "you're going straight to hell."

"I probably am," Hayes says, "but I've had fun while it's lasted. Speaking of fun, the bartender—the elegantly angular one, with the hair—his name is Bernie."

"People our age," Theresa says, "are actually named Bernie?"

"We rendezvoused in the pool area, if you can believe it, after you came up to the room to make the call I know you made and which I'm refusing to ask about on principle, because I don't want to hear about it, because I *told* you it was a bad idea. And still, you ignored me as if I had no valid input."

"You rendezvoused," Theresa says.

"Oh, I was safe," Hayes says, "If that's what you're thinking. Bernie and I will be meeting tonight after his shift for a little snip of something to drink, or several snips, or an entire bottle of snips, whatever happens. I'll need you gone, if you don't mind."

"Where will I *go*, if you don't mind?"

"You're a clever girl. You'll find somewhere. On our other matter of business, I was thinking we should go early, maybe do a little recon before our recon today."

She would like nothing more than to go back to sleep. She would like to sleep through these three days and be done with them—pack them up neatly, tuck them away. She does not know what she was thinking—what she wasn't thinking—when she agreed this idea was a good one, or at least an adequate one.

"We can do a drive-by," Hayes says. "Sit and look at the situation. Get a feel for things."

"When did you get so *militaristic*?"

"Gayness is all about clandestine operations. I thought you understood."

"I understand nothing," Theresa says.

Hayes agrees to drive if Theresa navigates. He crashes cars as if they are disposable, like toilet paper. He has a habit of constantly accelerating and braking as if he is never completely comfortable behind the wheel, or as if he'd like to wear his own grooves into the road, a sort of navigational trail of breadcrumbs. Also, she's never been a good navigator. She always fails to point out the turn, the juncture, the landmark. She goes west instead of east, north instead of south. She has a habit of driving forty miles past her exit before noticing the surrounding terrain looks subtly, imperceptibly different—the trees greener, the hills expanding at a sharper angle.

"I remember this," Theresa says as they cross the bridge into New Jersey. "I do."

"Nothing you say can comfort me right now," Hayes says, braking and accelerating.

Theresa crossed this bridge in her childhood. Her mother had driven her over this bridge in her long black Monte Carlo. Then, her mother had been bone-thin and beautiful, constantly fearful. She had countless nervous tics that Theresa suspected all mothers had. All mothers were, generally, neurotic: they trusted no one. They had faith in no one. It was something that happened to them during childbirth. Mothers locked doors and checked them twice. They looked over their shoulders; they did not make friends willingly; they folded under pressure. They kept things scrubbed and meticulous. They maintained a confined, manageable order. Her own mother cannot stand, never could stand, impulsiveness—impulsiveness of this specific variety, this driving over a bridge, this visiting a man she has not seen in years. Her mother does not like invitations to disaster. In general, she avoids them, just as she has taught Theresa to.

In New Jersey, when they've crossed over the border, Hayes says that he's going to stop, he wants something to eat. All they're doing, all they've done, Theresa observes, is eat.

"It quiets the nerves," Hayes says. "Really. It fattens them up, so they can't twang."

They stop at a diner that has music playing at each booth, crackling out of old speakers. Because she is here, in this remarkably foreign-feeling place, Theresa orders things she wouldn't normally consider: a cheeseburger cooked bloody rare, extra cheese, extra french fries, a large Coke. Everything around her, while not specifically dirty, suggests dirt. She doesn't actually find someone's hair on her plate, but it's like the waitress whisked the strand away at the last minute, before anyone noticed it.

"Tell me something before we see this old man, your father," Hayes says. "A memory, a story. Something before I meet him in the flesh."

She sucks at her Coke. "I've forgotten them or repressed them," she says. "Or maybe there aren't any. I'm not sure which."

"Seriously," Hayes says.

"I am serious."

"I was on *Oprah*," Hayes says abruptly.

"What?"

"I was," he says. "My mother recorded it when it aired. We have the VHS tapes, but I'll never show you."

"Of course not," Theresa says.

"If you must know, we haven't reached that level of *tenderness*. But anyway, this was back when I was really fat and always tucked my shirt into my pants, like, to my waist so that I looked like a little German kid who ate too much schnitzel or something."

"What," Theresa interrupts, "*is* schnitzel, actually?"

"I had a bowl cut up until the time I turned fourteen. I think my mother hoped I would become a child television star, because you know how they all happened to have bowl cuts. Anyway, I wasn't fourteen, I was maybe, like, seventeen, and I got tickets to *Oprah* because it was easy because I lived in Chicago, not because I especially liked her. My mother liked her, but she always reminded me of my most annoying aunt, who never let anyone else in on the conversation. I went with my friends, and unfortunately they were about as cool as I was. We got there, and Oprah had the audience fill out questionnaires about how much we lied—like, how many lies we told in a day, in a week, and what kinds of lies we told and what were the consequences of these lies. Had we *hurt* anyone with our lying? We had some time to fill out this thing, I don't remember how much, but I just made everything up. I said something crazy, like I'd told two hundred lies in a single week and that I'd hurt people with my lies and that my lies had tragic consequences."

"*Tragic consequences*," Theresa says. "It's, like, the title of a bad soap opera."

"The real story is this: later on, during the show, I wasn't even paying attention. I was probably sitting there picking at my skin or scraping off scabs because I was gross, then, always fidgeting with myself, and always embarrassing my parents, who made it a point to refrain from touching themselves—and I see my name on the teleprompter, and the next thing I know, Oprah's calling my name— my name—because she wants to talk to me about the exorbitant number of lies I tell. She says to me, *You're quite a liar. Two hundred lies in a week!* And I just stand there smiling, not able to say anything because this is Oprah, the Queen of Talk. I stood there for almost a full minute with this ridiculous smile on my face, and it was clear that even Oprah didn't know what to do with me right then. Even *Oprah* felt awkward. It was an utterly unfortunate moment."

"You're lying right now," Theresa says.

"Later it occurred to me that I should have just said, *It was a lie! I was lying!* That would have been brilliant. I'm always just a single step away from brilliance, but never actually brilliant. I've cheated myself out of countless small things like this, hundreds of little moments just like this one. Now, they're all merely anecdotal."

"You are lying," Theresa says, pushing her plate aside. Beside her, the waitress picks up their dishes with a heavy clatter, and Theresa has the feeling that Hayes is leading her somewhere, down some hazy path that she is too tired to follow.

"I swear to God," Hayes says. "I swear this is not a lie."

At her father's garage, Hayes announces himself to the receptionist: Hayes Cotter, oil change, checkup. Leaning toward the square cut into the wall, toward the woman who appears inside this square, Hayes makes small talk. Theresa scarcely listens to his elaborate prattle: long, dismal holiday drives; traffic and overcooked turkey. He's never been to New Jersey before, he's telling the receptionist, but his girlfriend has family here—at this moment Theresa jerks her head up before quickly jerking it back down—and he's with her now, visiting. The receptionist nods, blinks in response, taps her pen against the desktop. She has glorious cleavage but a poor attitude; this is, Theresa knows, a dangerous combination.

They sit on a rumpled couch to wait. Hayes wraps his arm around Theresa gently. "*Girlfriend,*" he whispers. His arm stays there, around her, like she's a throw pillow, while she pages through an automotive magazine. Looking at the sleek mechanical anatomy spread before her she feels schoolmarmish, too tailored and too plaid, too thick and wooly. She looks like a person who sleeps in hot rollers and who drives for breakfast croissants still dressed in a bathrobe. She is appreciative, anyway, to have Hayes beside her: handsome faux-boyfriend, sitting attentively at her elbow like a manicured pet. She sees him sneaking glances at the various mechanics as they pass.

"Will you recognize him?" he asks.

She studies a photograph of a contoured engine, shrugs. She has no idea. The receptionist shuffles her breasts around as if to organize them. Hayes twists into a more comfortable position on the couch. Classic rock plays on the stereo, a song Theresa's heard countless times, still can't identify, and which annoys her every time. They wait.

She sees him the exact moment he pushes through the swinging doors into the waiting area: sees him, in fact, and knows him. Immediately, she sits up straighter. She would like to seem the sort of person concerned with bone alignment, posture. She would like to seem a person who makes good first impressions.

As he approaches, her eyes go immediately to his face—does she see herself in him? His features appear decidedly sharpened, as if he is prepared, on a moment's notice, to extricate and use them as weapons. She has the quick image of her father, at night, whittling his cheekbone to a point as he watches *Wheel of Fortune*, drinking

Budweiser from twenty-four-ounce cans. His features are extreme enough to suggest he was once incredibly good-looking. He was once the thing women believe, when they are young, they need: a man who's angular and dangerous, intimidating. She forces herself to smile at him, the relaxed smile of someone who is resigned to a tedious day of errands but is sufficiently happy so as not to truly mind them, the smile of someone who enjoys making small talk with strangers. He frowns at her, as if he knows she's not this person.

"Hayes with the Prism?" he asks.

"It's Theresa with the Prism, actually," Hayes says. He has stood up and now gives a slight wave in Theresa's direction. Her father turns a bored expression on her. She holds her hand out for him to shake, and he turns his bored expression to the hand but doesn't shake it.

"*I'm* Theresa with the Prism," Theresa says, retracting her hand. She has not wanted to say this, but she has. Saying it, she has the awkward image of herself dressed in a white robe, standing on a hillside and holding a multicolored prism to the sun. She feels self-conscious, as if she's been caught wearing a dress entirely too small, or too frilly, or both. She considers, for a moment, bursting into nervous song.

"Whatever," her father says. "I'll tell both of you. You have transmission problems."

"I do?" Theresa asks.

"You do."

"Transmission problems," Theresa says. "Really."

Her father nods, looks away from her, at something on the wall. She follows his stare to an advertisement for engine lubricant, three cans of oil posed in an unhappy line like students in a grade-school recital.

"Transmissions are big," Theresa says. "Big and important, and big." She is throwing out words in an attempt to gain time, like someone throwing rocks to ward off a bully. She is, each time she opens her mouth, breathing him in as inconspicuously as she can manage. He smells like the interiors of things, like sweat and oil, dust. "Like, *expensive* big."

"Yes, darling, they're big," Hayes says. "You've mentioned that." He smiles at her father as if to suggest *silly girl*.

"It hasn't gone yet," her father says. "But it will. You're on the brink."

"The brink," she repeats and tries to imagine what, exactly, the brink looks like. It's a desert, she thinks, with little water and too much hot sand that burns her feet. She is looking sideways at Hayes in an attempt to understand how to handle this increasingly complicated situation. She was not expecting this curve. But Hayes is busily picking lint off his sweater as if this lint is the most tenacious of all lint. She knows perfectly well her car doesn't have a transmission problem. Or, she's relatively sure her car doesn't have a transmission problem. It could, possibly; she feels a whirligig of confusion. She changes her oil like she shaves her legs: barely. She scarcely knows the meaning of the word *maintenance*.

"To know for sure," her father says, "I would need to look at things, take the transmission out."

"That's extreme," she says. "Considering."

She wants him to ask, considering what? She imagines her response: *we haven't come here, actually, for the car,* though she's unsure what would follow. *Do you really want to fuck over your daughter?* Her father shrugs, and all at once, his presence—his unfaltering apathy—unnerves her. His ribs, visible beneath the threadbare t-shirt he's wearing, unnerve her. The peculiar light blue of his eyes unnerves her. She feels as if she's dropped pieces of herself into her own engine, and these pieces—her oversized hips and thighs, her neck that seems unnaturally thick, her shoulders that seem freakishly wide—have clogged everything up.

"I'm busy today," he says. "I can't do it today."

"Of course," Theresa says. "It's, like, a holiday. A time for family and reflection."

Her father stares at her.

"Right," Hayes says, looking sideways at them both, and Theresa understands that this is the moment, according to Hayes's grandiose plan, for the surprise—the unveiling, the *ta-da*, the *pièce de résistance*. But she is realizing that she has known, all along, that she would let this moment go untouched, unscathed. She has known that she would reject this moment, just as she knows it is important to be the rejecter of things rather than the rejected. This is a lesson she learned early on, back when she was a fourth grader with oversized breasts wearing bobos and sweatpants and mucking up all the big plays in gym class.

Her father is saying something about a teardown while Theresa fumbles through her bag as though for something necessary. She doesn't wear lipstick, doesn't even own any, but she searches for it intently at the bottom of her bag. She fumbles, and while her head is bent down like this, Hayes manages one awkward kiss on the back of her neck. His lips remain, waiting, at the edge of her hairline, and in this instant her father leaves, swings through the doors into the garage with the same nonchalance with which he entered, and Theresa grasps that her moment—the threshold of this opportunity—has come and gone. Like her earring holes, like an ant mound she's kicked at, it has closed up. The receptionist nods to her expectantly. Hayes's lips leave the back of her neck. And then, she pays.

At the hotel, they drink.

Hayes orders her a bourbon, neat. "I'm sorry," Hayes says. "I am."

The lights inside the bar are dim yet piercing. She sees sunspots, as if someone has just snapped her picture, and she knows it's a picture she'd rather not see.

"There's no need for that," she says.

He says, "The doctor called me, you know."

For a moment all that exists between them is the bar's background music, ill-conceived and dreamy, suggestive of quiet undulating paisley.

"Right," he says. "I forgot. I'll undo the little lies I've told and tell you that, actually, I took the test two weeks ago, and in the last week the doctor has called me three times asking me to call him at home. There, now you're up to speed. I thought maybe you'd have put two and two together. I haven't called him back." He pauses, taps at the stem of his glass. "You know what that means, a phone call. It's like when you're young and the principal calls. He never calls about anything good. He just wants to tell you, in a methodical list, all the things you haven't done right recently, and all the things you'll never do right."

"He's thorough," Theresa says. "He likes to follow through. It's what he learned in med school about giving proper care. Ha!" she says. "Proper care."

"You call people when there's something to tell. He has his sad little birdsong to sing, and he needs to do it person to person." Hayes shrugs. "That's his line. It isn't his fault. I'll call him later. I need some time to be normal, the way I think normal is before it's not normal. I just want to smoke, and he might tell me I can't do that anymore, it's *bad* for me."

"It's bad for you anyway," Theresa says.

"Whatever. I need to smoke, and this bar doesn't have ashtrays, like it's too good for smoke, it's fucking *above* smoke. We don't live in California," Hayes says. "Here, we smoke in bars. It's what we do."

They find themselves, by default, at the pool area.

Theresa lights Hayes's cigarette, and they stand at the edge of the hot tub, balancing their drinks in the cold and staring at the water.

"Come on," Hayes is suddenly saying, handing his cigarette to her and stripping off his clothes, peeling them off as if to get to the bottom of something. He doesn't bother folding anything. He kicks his pants, his boxers, off into the distance.

"You just can't keep them on," she says.

"I can't," he says. He stands naked, shivering, before her, and she returns his cigarette to him. "It's a problem. It's proven to be a problem."

He steps carefully into the hot tub: first one toe, then a second toe, ankles, thighs, hips. He holds his cocktail in his right hand, balancing it.

"*Do Not Consume Alcoholic Beverages While Using the Tub*," she reads.

"You're so antiquated," Hayes tells her. "If I pass out, I'm certain you'll save me."

"Don't be sure," she says.

"Come on," he says. "Make the most of your amenities."

The water has encompassed him like something greedy. He tilts his head backward. His uncomplicated breathing, his easy sprawl, encourage her. She does away with the top layers quickly—her woolen jacket, her pinstriped shirt. She stands at the edge of the hot tub wearing only her underwear and bra. "Off with everything," he says, and averts his eyes as she, too, kicks her undergarments out of her temporary grasp into the darkness. He reaches his hand to help her.

Inside, she relaxes slightly. "It's nice, I guess. I think."

"Sometimes," Hayes says, "I wish I were still fat. Like, really fat. I might have had a different future, a different *kind* of homosexuality—role-playing games, *Dungeons and Dragons*, constant shyness. I'd be an engineer and speak Klingon and attend sci-fi conventions and dress up in garb."

"I don't think so," Theresa says. Inside the safety of the water, she can't help it—she touches her breasts, and it comes to her: her breasts, the newfound padding on her hips and thighs, is her body providing a means of protection, a means of resilience against countless unfavorable emotions, countless unfavorable events. She is no longer so thin that even the easy things can break her.

"I could have been a person like that," Hayes says.

"You're a person like this," she says, and she kisses Hayes right below the edge of his cheekbone. He has a beautiful cheek, smooth, which he tilts toward her. They meet in the middle, lips and cheek, like the perfect crease of a folded page. "We're people like this," she says, even while hoping that someone, watching them, could misread them for something entirely different from who and what they are. In this moment, they are willing. They are not impervious to care. They are, neither of them, afraid of tenderness. They are not afraid to succumb, just succumb.

# ACKNOWLEDGMENTS

Thank you to the editors who helped make these stories their best selves and who gave them their first homes. Thank you, always, to Lena Bertone, for reading every word and for having the innate knack for telling me either yes or no. Thank you to my parents, who got me through unscathed. Thank you to the restaurants I've called my second homes and to the good people I've worked with and for. (Rich Wood and Roger Feuer, I'm looking at you.)

Shane. You are a man of few words. I am verbose. Who knew what a perfect union it would be?

Stories in this volume initially appeared in *Cincinnati Review* ("Lessons in Geography," "Myths of the Body," "Monsieur"), *Confrontation* ("American Silk"), *Gettysburg Review* ("*Paradiso nel Frigorifero*"), *Gulf Coast* ("Brethren"), *Juked* ("Narrative Time"), *Los Angeles Review* ("Her Adult Life"), and *Santa Monica Review* ("Care").